The Imaginary Wizard

PHILLIP VAIRA

To St. Monica's middle
School,

Phil Vaira

Summary:

From the ashes of tragedy, a young boy will find the courage to survive. Eons in the future amid the ruins of civilization, Alex, an eleven year old, spends his days cleaning chimneys for his village — when he isn't sneaking off to play imaginary games as the Greatest and Bravest Wizard in the world. When his village is destroyed by the brutal Lord Mallis, Alex sets off on a real adventure — a quest for revenge. His childlike innocence at stake, fantasy and reality collide as the remarkable boy traverses the treacherous land, facing dangers both real and imagined. With help from his friends, Alex proves that even mighty empires can't escape justice.

Copyright © 2015 Phillip Vaira
Illustrations by Bruce Brenneise copyright © 2015 by
Phillip Vaira
Edited by Alex Bostwick
Graphic Design by Ron Marshall

ISBN: 1530355338
ISBN-13: 978-1530355334

www.ImaginaryWizard.com

NOVELS BY PHILLIP VAIRA

The Imaginary Wizard

FILMS BY PHILLIP VAIRA

The Sandwich Days

A Hero's Gift

To my mom,
Patricia Ward,
while still feeling her ongoing
love and support from above.

CONTENTS

CHAPTER 1
THE BOX OF CRRR

There once lived the greatest and bravest wizard of them all. No matter where one would visit, everyone knew and feared this one, rather short hero: Alex, a ten-year-old.

Now don't let the wizard's age fool you. As powerful and glorious as the imaginative boy was, Alex still had to return to the regular boring tasks of real life in the deep woods, such as attending school, taking care of his grandfather, and working in his small hamlet. At other times—during his work breaks or when sneaking off—he'd be happily playing. Sometimes he'd end up in a situation that is not so glorious or fun, like being taken prisoner in a creepy, deep underworld.

This was one of those times.

Alex squinted his eyes to get a better look around him. The cave was dark and still. The airshaft from above provided enough light to remind him of his dirty rags, grimy skin, the dirt-filled ground he sat on, and the aged iron bars that locked him within the lonely chamber. It was anything but a good place to celebrate his eleventh birthday, which was next week.

The airshaft's hint of fresh air helped Alex forget the foul, lingering odor. The stench made Alex want to climb up the airshaft, but its thin tunnel mocked his size.

Young, equally unlucky captives cried in the distance. Their sobs echoed down the tunnels, drowning out the sound of dripping water. With a timid breath, Alex pulled his trembling knees up to his chest and lowered his reddening head. His shoulders quaked as he sobbed and sniffled.

"Alex?" a soft voice whispered ahead, possibly from a young girl. "Is it truly the greatest and bravest wizard of them all?"

Alex gasped, and lifted his head. He squinted his bleary eyes toward the bars. Unable to see the person's face, Alex wiped away his tears and leaned to his side. Yes, a small, darkened figure stood behind the bars! She was about Alex's height, with long, tangled hair.

Alex asked with a shaky voice, "Who's there?"

The figure's round cheeks rose in a smile. "Well, it's the second greatest and bravest wizard you've ever known."

"Anne!" Alex scrambled upward. He sprinted toward the bars, casting soft dirt from between his toes. "How?" he asked, gripping the cold iron. "I mean... how did you escape from the goblins?"

"Well, I guess I can tell you." Anne said, sitting down in a comfy spot. "What a long story, though! Where to begin? As you know, we were searching for the dagger..."

"The enchanted dagger of Ephacotus?"

"You do know how nerdy that just sounded, right?" Anne jibed, smirking. "Anyway, let me finish my story! So we were trying to find it. And then... we were captured in this cave. And then... what a long story, though! Let me tell..."

"Never mind that!" Alex shouted, gripping the bars tighter. "Get me out of here!"

"So I got my tunic dirty just for that?" Anne stood as she brushed the long cloth. "Whatever."

"We need to finish our mission," Alex said. His eyes veered upward. "I was thinking where we should check next. We were in the east, right? I think we covered all of that, so if we go west now..."

Alex caught Anne smirking widely once more. She slowly pulled out a sharp, medium-sized object.

Alex stared at the item, his jaw dropping open. "Is

that the dagger?"

"Duh," Anne said, lifting her nose. "It looks pretty when it's under some light. There's some strange carving along the steel. You can't really see it from here. It looked like big letters. Wait!" She looked closer at the carving. "Got it! Are you ready? It reads, 'Alex is a dork for getting us caught.'"

"Really funny," Alex muttered.

"Why were we searching for the dagger again?" Anne asked.

"To destroy the Box of *Crrr*."

"What's that?"

His eyes fell as he shuffled his feet through the loose dirt. "You wouldn't understand."

Anne placed her hands on her hips. "So I came all the way down here with you, and you won't tell me what the Box of *Crrr* is?"

"Please," Alex said with clenched teeth, "just open the lock!"

"Okay... okay." Anne sighed. "You may be the greatest and bravest, but you sure are the most impatient-*est*, if that's a word. Here you go."

Anne pointed her wand toward the cell's rusty keyhole. "What was that spell again? I always forget what it is." Her eyes widened. "Oh! Abracadabra!"

The lock clicked; its loud echo flew past Anne and sailed through the cave's long-winded tunnels.

"Oops. That can't be good." Anne promptly faced Alex. "Never mind that! Come! I know the way out."

Anne stretched her right hand through the closed bars, grabbed Alex's closest hand, turned, and dashed forward. After a few steps, a loud clunk rumbled the bars. Alex fell with a daze.

Anne's eyes widened.

"Oh my gosh!" Anne rushed back to Alex. "What was I thinking? Are you all right?"

"I'm doing great!" Alex said sarcastically.

While the room spun out of control, Alex caught Anne sliding the gate open. The gate's stubbornness took her entire—though surprising—strength.

"Yes, a girl rescued you," Anne said with a pleased smile. "Remember me if you write an account or a book one day. And make me stronger… and prettier. Though maybe not the way I have my hair right now. It's been so dirty and tangled these days at home. You know, like yours. Also, if you can…"

"Anne!" Alex yelled.

"Oh, right! Come!"

Taking Anne's hand, Alex stood up, stepped out of the chamber, and followed her into total darkness. Unaware of his surroundings, he bashed his left arm against the wall. Loose dirt tumbled to the ground.

"It's too dark," Alex complained. "I can't see."

"No problem," Anne said, straightening her posture. "That's what this wand is for! Abracadabra!" A bright, sparkling light flourished from the wand, revealing an extensive, jagged tunnel.

Anne shouted from ahead, "It's down here!"

While they rushed down the tunnel, a splitting shriek echoed from behind. They froze and stared at each other with wide eyes.

"Was that your stomach?" Anne asked.

Anne shrugged, and then walked onward.

Alex trembled where he stood. He knew that horrifying, screechy sound all too well; it had always made the hairs on the back of his neck stand straight up. Biting a quivering lip, he slowly turned around.

A dark figure, about half of Alex's size, stood there with pointy ears, a hint of green skin, and glowing eyes. The figure slowly walked toward them, favoring its right leg. A few other elder goblins crawled into sight.

"Goblins!" Alex yelled, pointing a shaking finger toward them. "Run!"

With every step, their heartbeats hammered in their ears, but it didn't drown out the vibrating steps of the goblins, whose thundering footfalls shook their spines. Alex dared to glance over his shoulder, catching glimpses of their pursuers close behind. Breathlessly, he turned back to Anne who rushed toward a gap of light. And then he realized there was no further point in running—they had reached a dead end.

"Now what?" Alex yelled. "You can shoot the goblins, right?"

"Well, yes," said Anne, "but it wouldn't be quite as dramatic."

Alex jerked his head back. "What? Wait, I'm the bravest. I say we fight!"

Anne rolled her eyes, clearly accustomed to Alex's straightforward suggestions. She shook her head, and replied, "You're not being so brave today, so we climb!"

"Climb what?" Alex asked.

Anne pointed above them. "Up there, of course!"

Alex craned his neck to follow her finger, chewing on his lip. A long-tunneled borehole stretched upward for about five hundred feet. At the top, he could see the pale blue sky. An aged rope hung from top to bottom—odd, yet convenient.

"Better start climbing," Anne said, "or you'll be on the goblins' menu for dinner!"

Anne stretched her hand as high as she could, grasped the rope, and began to climb. She climbed easily, her hands and bare feet gripping the rope tightly and securely.

Already regretting this plan, Alex grabbed the rope with a trembling hand. His eyes veered upward as his jaw grew heavy.

"There's no way I can climb that high," Alex insisted, shaking his head slowly.

"Why?" Anne asked.

"I'm afraid of heights!"

"Since when is a wizard afraid of heights?" Anne asked. "Come on! Brave it out!"

Alex needed motivation to climb something so high. A goblin stormed toward him, which provided plenty motivation. With widened eyes, Alex turned to the rope and climbed hurriedly.

"Give me your wand!" Alex shouted from ten feet off the ground.

"Why?" Anne said, glaring downward. "It's not my fault you lost yours!"

"Hurry!" Alex yelled.

Anne sighed. "Fine."

Anne dropped her wand. Alex caught it deftly. He

pointed the wand at the goblin below, and shouted, "Abracadabra!"

A raging fireball burst from the wand, striking it straight in the chest. The goblin only whined and hissed, and then glared upward, eyes narrowing. The goblin jumped higher, trying to reach Alex.

"Faster!" Alex yelled, firing again and again. "Abracadabra! Abracadabra! Why does it take so long to say the word ABRACADABRA?"

"I'm trying to climb faster!" Anne yelled. "If it weren't for you and your grandfather's cooking last night…"

The goblin leaped even higher. Its scaly hand grasped onto Alex's ankle.

"Help!" Alex squealed.

With only one thing left to do, Alex kicked the goblin's face as hard as he could. The goblin just lowered its head, and ground its teeth. It gripped Alex's ankle even tighter, sinking its claws into his skin.

Alex sank down the rope. The rope burned his hand as he slid, inch by inch. He couldn't hold on much longer. One finger came loose, then another, and another, until he had no other choice but to let go.

Alex fell, scraping himself and hitting his head against the borehole's dirt walls—which strangely felt like brick walls—until billows of ash fogged his sight. Having landed on Anne's wand—which strangely felt like his familiar sweeping brush—he coughed out ash, turned to his side, and coughed some more.

The boy was not eaten up by the goblin; he lay on the bottom of a chimney. Soot and ash caked his skin. Sitting up from the debris and ash, Alex looked beyond his sole, soot-tainted waistcloth. His injured ankle had no cuts—not even a single scratch.

Just above the ash clouds at the top of the chimney, longing swirled in Alex's eyes as he saw the pale blue sky once again.

Down below, Alex knew his customer's home and fireplace all too well. Returning to what his grandfather called *the real world* made him sigh. Alex admitted he had a tendency to daydream and pretend to be somewhere else, especially when he had to climb up dark, spooky chimneys to sweep them clean. The work life was a harsher reality than the heroic, adventurous life he had always craved.

The wooden living room was to Alex's left. A blazing light shined through its glassless windows, making Alex squint his eyes against the glare. At the far right corner of the room, his only ragged outfit hung on a pole hanger. A dusty piano stood nearby, against the right wall. At the other end, a tattered, faded flag of red, white, and blue hung. A white robotic puppy cowered behind an aged couch. It peeked at Alex behind its shiny blue paws and nose. Sitting on the couch were two elders in animal hides. They relaxed their stiffened postures.

The male elder, who favored his right leg, lowered his cracked glasses. He glanced at his wife and laughed, "After talking with himself, the imaginary wizard took his fall! We might have to go with an imaginary chimneysweeper now!"

Alex rolled his eyes and closed them tightly. He wished he could go back to his daydreaming and live a heroic life, but his adventure fled from him until only darkness remained. Alex coughed out another thick cloud of ash.

CHAPTER 2
LIFE IN THE WOODS

L ife wasn't fair. Work was for grownups—or so
Alex wished. He just wanted to be like the
traditional kids that he learned about in his history
lessons, kids who went to school and played afterward.
Instead, his dreams of play and adventure led to
mockery from the adults. Alex never understood why
this was so. What could possibly be wrong with a child
adventuring deep into the woods to play as a wizard,
fighting ferocious monsters lurking within?

Adults needed to back off.

Sure, Alex's grandfather and other elders warned
him of deadly monsters that lived deep in the woods,
and they didn't mean bears, wolves, or other natural
forest creatures; rather, they said certain monsters
specialized in hunting down adventurous children.

The elders warned,

> *If you disturb them and turn pulp,*
> *You'll be their supper with one gulp!*

Thus, the only allowable adventure for Alex was a
ten-minute walk to the local river to either clean up or
gather water. Boring! Even so, the river became Alex's
quiet place, one that begged him to visit all morning

long.

Underneath several blooming trees, through the thick fog, Alex raced his white terrier down a well-trodden path. Alex's tough-skinned feet felt no pain over the path's dirt and rocks; rather, he chuckled and beamed from ear to ear. His dog raced ahead of him with small flapping ears and bouncing fur.

"You won't beat me to the river!" Alex shouted with a smile.

There was plenty to smile about outside of dark, creepy chimneys; the early spring air smelled fresh and crisp, the birds sang in testimony of their freedom, and Alex could enjoy his favorite subject of science by the river.

The clear, shallow water of the river drew closer. The sound of the running water was soothing and spellbinding. The riverbed twisted like the garter snake Alex once found slithering in the grass.

After reaching the river, Alex observed the water's reflection. It gave the images a whitened haze, one that swallowed up the tall evergreen trees mirrored on its surface. Alex's smile withered away as he bit his lip, and moved closer to his rippling likeness depicted in the water.

Alex knelt at the river's edge. Taking a deep breath, he closed his eyes and leaned forward. He imagined looking down to see a reflection of a boy hero with a wizard's robe and pointed hat. Fearing the worst, Alex bravely opened his eyes and observed the water's reflection. His light brown hair, both tousled and overgrown, lay haphazardly across his brow; its stringy strands reached midway down his ears. Unfortunately, his hair did little to hide the tainted soot smudged about his face and neck.

Shaking his head, Alex cupped his hands and filled them with water. He rubbed the water against his face. With little luck, some of the soot washed off. He scrubbed even harder. His reflection continued to show darkened soot about his face, which reminded him that his break time from work was nearly over.

Alex's cheeks grew red, and his lips tightened.

His tears mixed with the water, and swam freely down the stream.

***

"Hold on, Max," Alex said a few hours later near the waterbed.

Alex leaned against an evergreen tree while Max, his dog and only audience, tilted his furry, dirt-caked head. Alex reached into a half-ripped pocket in his baggy, cut-off trousers. "I'm going to show you what we wizards use to fight," Alex said with gleaming eyes. "First, we need to craft it. Here's one of our top-secret tools." Alex pulled out a rusty pair of children's scissors.

Alex dropped to his knees and crossed his legs. "Okay. Next, we need some cotton."

Licking his lips, Alex moved the scissors toward his worn shirt. The shirt appeared to have once been longer; its bottom had several rectangular cuts. His short black cloak, pinned at his right shoulder, hid most of the cuts. He cut a strip of the shirt's cloth carefully from the bottom, just as straight-lined as the other previous cuts. After a careful study of the strip, Alex gave a crisp nod.

"Then we need to do this," Alex said, rolling the cotton strip into a ball. Next, he reached into a pocket and pulled out a thin needle with a cotton string attached, and he wrapped it around the ball until it tightened.

The next step was to use the mysterious, magical liquid his father had bought from a traveling trader. The fluid made everyone nervous, but Alex was a professional. He knew the villagers would come to him one day to get expert advice and support with what he considered real science. With such great respect, they may let him go from his work duties.

Until then, Alex's dog supported him. Max wagged his tail, anticipating whatever Alex had secretly planned.

"Just a few more seconds. Okay, Max?" Alex said. He pulled out a small, dirt-stained bottle from another pocket. "It's worth waiting for. It will be the most wicked fire trick you will ever see! I swear! Now listen closely. This trick can happen only with this type of cloth, and —"

"Woof!" the dog barked.

"What?" Alex followed Max's wide eyes down to what he held: it was the newly formed cotton ball. "Oh, you want the ball? You want to play fetch?"

Max leaned against his front legs and let out another big "Woof!"

Alex grinned. He sat upright, dug his bare right heel into the ground, and threw the cotton ball with all his strength. Max stormed off with little legs pumping furiously, and soon enough he hurried back with the ball secured in his mouth. After taking the ball, Alex watched Max lean in again.

Alex pursed his lips, tilted his head, and then asked, "Have you ever chased a flaming ball?"

"Woof!" the dog barked loudly.

Encouraged by the reply, Alex poured the container's liquid onto the cotton ball. He took his lighter out. It was red, white, and blue, but the colors were faded, washed out over time. He flicked it a few times. Eventually, a short spark of fire burst out. Alex moved the lighter toward the ball, met the fire with the cotton, and then the ball burst into a big flame! But it did not hurt Alex's hand. He closed his hand, covering the flame, and when he opened his hand again the flame reappeared!

"Isn't that cool?" Alex asked with intense eye contact. "You see, this kind of cloth doesn't hurt you, unless you touch the top of the flame. So you don't want to touch there unless you're really asking for it."

"Woof!" Max barked with total understanding.

"Yeah, I know!" Alex said, his shoulders set back with pride. "Are you ready? Fetch this!"

Beaming widely, Alex threw the fireball down the forest path. Max dashed towards it. When Max reached the landing spot along the trail, he stopped and stared at the flaming ball. His wide eyes turned to Alex, who fell to the ground with laughter.

***

"Thanks for watching my science trick, Max," Alex said minutes later as they climbed up a small, damp hill. "No one else cares about my tricks. There was my dad, but... well, you know what happened."

Alex's dropped his gaze sadly, only to raise his eyebrows as he recalled Max's youthfulness. "Or were you there when I was six? He burned our home down, and then the hamlet kicked him out!"

Max's tongue hopped about as he gazed adoringly up at Alex.

"I know!" Alex said. "Grandpa said it was for some other reason. He thinks I'm too young to know why. I'm not a little kid anymore! I'm eleven next week, you know. Now it's only you who cares about my tricks.

"Well," he continued, maneuvering his foot away from a slimy slug on the ground below, "there was Jack from the next hamlet over. Do you remember him? We used to pretend to be wizards, but then his mom and dad freaked out when I was showing him fireballs in my hands. They said I was 'in sync with evil spirits.' That's dumb! I don't even know what that means!"

Alex was still puzzled by Jack's parents and the distant memory of them running around in circles, afraid, but still screaming endless generalizations, until Max ran around in circles with them just for the fun of it. The memory ceased when Alex and Max reached the top of the hill.

Through the chill, cloaking fog, several wooden, rope-tied roofs came into view ahead of them. Alex's lips twitched, struggling to smile.

A few steps further improved the view of the hamlet. It had eight log-built homes and one bulky inn. Each building had pale shades of brown, and their roofs were triangular, topped with rugged wooden boards. Glassless windows used fur cloths as shutters. Each building had a chimney that waited eagerly for Alex, minus the few he had already cleaned. Trees circled the hamlet's local field and its few vegetable gardens, and a tall cliff ahead overlooked the whole area.

While walking closer, Alex found the usual activity going on. A few villagers, barefoot and wearing timeworn tunics, tilled the gardens. Nearby, a tall, heavy-set man chopped away at a fallen log—Alex's eyes glanced away. That's when he spotted Mrs. Pembleton—a tall, strict elder—leaving her home. She had curly gray hair, which hid several worn lines on her long cheeks. Alex couldn't help but grin, thinking of some of his treasured memories with her.

Mrs. Pembleton would often grumble when she found Alex with one of his troubling fire tricks. She would often shout the familiar phrase, "Children shouldn't play with fire!" Reporting Alex did no good, as the villagers tended to shrug it off. That may feel odd, but most of the hamlet had benefited from what

Alex called science.

Science, though seldom practiced in the hamlet's local woods, had caused some trouble in the past. For instance, Mrs. Pembleton shared stories of the helpless hamlet scorching in fire and toppling over, insisting that only a few people had fled in time to save their lives. Everyone found that strange, however, because the hamlet was still there. She was convinced it happened, but the villagers simply let her go with a gentle pat on the shoulder.

If one really wanted to know what took place with Alex's accidents, it was best to look to the other villagers. They would only share of minor accidents, such as when Alex set a barrel on fire… or when he set his own hair on fire—no known magic could help Alex forget *that* event.

Chimneys, though dreadful the cleaning was, remained one of Alex's fond memories with his father. They reinvented fireplaces, said to warm ancient houses. They used a small wooden block for a switch. When the switch was turned, it would tug a rope to begin a new fire. What Alex *didn't* like was everyone's belief that they had to maintain and clean each chimney flue, as if that were part of the contract!

Another grumbler, though not as bad, appeared near the inn, and he gave Alex a wide wave. His name was Mr. Nutter, a peaceful elder, who had never spoken a single word. The nutty part was that the silence didn't prevent him from showing his disapproval, often by giving a slow shake of his head with his index finger swaying from left to right. Even when Alex *thought* about pulling out his fire tools from his rope belt or his half-ripped pockets, there was Mr. Nutter with that finger again. And now it was in his head and in his dreams—make it stop!

At the same time, Alex knew Mr. Nutter enjoyed the surrounding forest as much as he did. It was a place of happiness and freedom, but that happiness faded as the trees thinned with each step, tree stumps and two gardens taking their place.

"Oh, thank goodness!" A gardener shouted, storming toward Alex.

Alex's eyes widened; he must have passed the field's peaceful line divider.

The woman's reddened face had long blond hair tied from behind. Alex wished he had something to tie her hands at the moment as she fiercely pointed at him. She yelled, "Alex, tell your grandfather, George, to turn that maddening noise box down! I swear my daughter and I can hear that noise from here, and it's driving us, well, mad!"

"It's not really that bad, Mother," a twelve-year-old girl said from behind the woman as she petted Max. Her familiar face, although a year older than in Alex's daydreams, grinned at Alex. "And it's called a radio. I'm used to it."

"Don't listen to Anne," the mother blurted. She

narrowed her eyes at Anne, only to widen them as her daughter returned the same expression. "Oh my, she is turning into me, and here I was deeply worried.

"Alex," Anne's mother sighed, "I tried knocking and your grandfather won't answer! He's going deaf with that thing! As I said before, you need to stop playing and start taking care of your grandfather."

Alex lowered his eyes. "Sorry, ma'am."

Anne's mother was right. The radio noise wasn't the first complaint against his grandfather—maybe the thousandth?

"You will tell him, right?" she asked.

Alex nodded, studying the tall green grass. "Yes."

"Great!" The mother smiled, resting her hands on her waist. "One less empire toy makes a happier hamlet. So how goes your day?"

Alex shrugged, unsure whether to talk about the work he had to do but loathed, or how he had relaxed by the river when he should have been preparing for school at noon. He mumbled, "Well, I was..."

"That's wonderful, dear!" the mother interrupted. "Now go along and tell him this instant!" She turned and faced the garden.

Alex raised an eyebrow. "Um, okay."

Come to think of it, Anne's mother had always been an odd sort. She allowed the children to call her by her first name, Helen. Doing so caused uproar around the hamlet, until it found something else to be angry about. She was quite the mix of perky and agitated. Her voice rose in those confusing, emotional town meetings, yet she always hummed peacefully when she worked in the gardens—well, besides the days when static noise blared throughout the field.

Her daughter always smiled, though, which went well with her rosy round cheeks and long blonde hair. It made Alex forget about her rugged, brown-stained tunic that just didn't quite seem to suit her. If they could adventure outward and buy new clothes in the Empire's cities legally, she'd become the most beautiful... wait—yuck! What was he thinking?

Alex missed playing wizards with Anne. They both had their work duties, and so Alex would just daydream new adventures as he remembered her younger self. He wanted to play with her. His lips formed to say something, but then—just a few houses away—he heard a cringing, ear-twitching noise.

***

Moments later, Alex opened a thin, uneven door. The radio's static noise grew tenfold. The door's hinges appeared loose, but then again, loose things were commonplace in such homes. Perhaps all homes in the world had cold, frail floors that creaked, too. Alex preferred to be outside to avoid floor splinters, but most of all to avoid the blaring static noise just up ahead.

The noise came from the only wooden table. Nails

stuck out from the table's legs—Alex wouldn't admit who fixed it.

An elderly man sat behind the table. His long gray hair and beard matched his lengthy animal hides. A used, dark-green army hat topped his head. He kept his eyes down, listening to the static noise that *CRRR'ed* out from the radio.

"Hi, Grandpa," Alex shouted.

CRRR...

His grandfather looked up, startled and wincing, and shouted, "What?"

CRRR...

Alex roared louder, "I said 'hi!'"

CRRR...

George cupped his right ear with a wrinkled hand. "What?"

The corner of Alex's eye caught something startling. He jumped, seeing a figure's large and pointy nose, gigantic eyes, and an evil grin that greeted him from its place next to the door. It was one of his grandfather's recent wood-carved statues: a goblin, he called it.

How Alex wished his grandfather wouldn't place his woodcarvings in the most unexpected places! He thought his grandfather did it just to mess with him— his grandfather was good at it, after all. He liked to carve wood. The raw logs he started with turned into human bodies, tree monsters, trolls, or other frightening monsters with strange, goofy faces and sometimes even very dark, scary faces with haunted eyes and evil grins.

This statue reminded Alex of an event he tried to forget. One night he woke up from blinding lightning and deafening thunder. When the lightning flashed, he saw a huge statue of a terrifying tree monster next to his bed! He remembered throwing blankets over himself. It was like a nightmare, but his grandfather claimed the wooden statue was a birthday present for him. Alex didn't know what was in his grandfather's head, but he'd rather stay out of it. Maybe it was due to the...

CRRR...

Shaking his head, Alex furrowed his eyebrows and pointed sternly at the radio. "Grandpa! Turn it down!"

CRRR...

"What?" George yelled.

CRRR…

"Turn it down!" Alex shouted.

Finally, George nodded and fumbled around for the power button. When the *CRRRing* stopped, Alex could have sworn he heard villagers clapping outside.

Alex sighed deeply as he relaxed his fists. He walked closer to the table, and said in a sharp tone, "Grandpa, Helen is mad because you keep turning your radio up. You need to keep it down!"

"But I… I just heard something on there… after all these years." George's eyes gazed upward, gleaming. "Do you hear a ringing in the air?"

"There's nothing on there!" Alex said, annoyed. "It's just static noise like the last three years of my life!"

"Oh, no, my grandson," George said, shaking his head. "Someone was talking about Ancient America!"

"America?" Alex tilted his head. The corner of his left eye caught an aged and tattered flag on the wooden wall with faded colors of red, white, and blue. "You really heard something on there?"

"Sure as ever!" George said as he patted the radio. His army hat slipped further to one side. "Or was it about New France? I…"

"Just keep it down," Alex said with a heavy sigh. He fell back onto a crooked chair. "And voices don't come out of nowhere. I hate solar power, or whatever it is."

"What's the matter, Alex?"

Alex's eyes locked onto the front door. "Nothing."

"Well, I may be forgetful at times, but I can tell when you get upset."

"You're embarrassing me!"

"Embarrassing you? No!" George shook his head, and then froze, his eyes wide. "Oh..."

Alex raised a brow at George. "What?"

"I've seen this before." George rubbed his chin. "This resentment... Yes, yes, when your father was your age, maybe a year or two older! Quite the little rebel, I'd say. Very into appearance, and what people thought of him—all part of becoming a man."

"Grandpa, I'm ten."

"Yes, yes, almost eleven by next week, and that's when it nearly begins!"

"What begins?"

A stern voice rumbled from his grandfather's straight face. "Puberty."

"Oh my God."

"You know what your father and I did?"

Alex gulped. "I'm afraid to ask."

"We put it in the back of our minds and totally forgot about it," George said with a knowing nod. "Trust me; it was far, far better that way. We just took our hiking sticks and ended up spending quality father-son time together. Problem solved!"

Alex sunk deeper in his chair. "Oh great."

"You and I..." George trailed off, rubbing his chin.

"We'll go camping up on the hill tonight. Just you and I."

"I'd rather stay here."

"No, no. After all, as part of becoming a man," George pointed at the spine-tingling statue by the door, "it's about time you learn what happened to your parents."

Alex's face lit up. At the same time, the statue's sharp teeth made his mouth fall wide open.

"We leave at sunset." George stood up with the table's support. "Just remind me what we're doing after your duties today. My memory hasn't been so great lately. Oh my, how long have I been sitting here?"

CHAPTER 3
A NEW SCIENCE "TOY"

Alex lifted the axe high into the air. His eyes locked onto a bulky log below, which waited for a final swing.

Whoosh! The blade smashed into the log. The last six-inch portion cracked and toppled onto the grass.

Alex carefully kicked the two pieces into the large pile with the rest. He wiped sweat off his forehead, only to find his hand smeared with soot. Alex hoped by the end of work he'd be too tired for the dreaded camping with his grandfather. Then again, he felt eager to learn what happened to his parents.

"Mr. Smith!" Alex shouted.

Setting aside the wood axe, Alex reached for his cloak on a low tree branch. Before he could grab it, someone shouted from behind, "Well, look at that!"

Alex spun around.

Mr. Smith stood there in his sleeveless animal hides. He rested his hands on his waist and lifted his chin high. His closed-mouth smile hid behind the disheveled red hair and beard, only to relax Alex when his teeth parted with a firm nod.

"I finished, sir," Alex said, shoulders back. "May I

be excused now?"

"Marvelous!" Mr. Smith cheered as he walked closer. "Look at you! You're getting some real-world experience in you! How was your first week of woodcuttin'?"

"It was hard, but fun, too," Alex said. "I got to leave school early for the assignment."

Mr. Smith laughed as he crossed his arms. "Is it still three hours a day in class?"

Alex nodded.

"Back in my day, it was..." Mr. Smith's eyes locked onto something below. He slowly dropped his arms to his side. "Oh dear."

"What?" Alex followed Mr. Smith's gaze to the woodpile. He rubbed his mud-spattered foot against his leg.

"The firewood..." Mr. Smith leaned in closer. "They look six inches."

Alex gulped. "That's what you wanted. Right?"

"Twelve inches!" Mr. Smith scoffed, facing Alex again. "But never mind about that. The important thing is you're getting some real-world experience with your woodcuttin'. Then you will be out of here. And then I can drink the finest drink in all the land!" He paused, scratching his head. "Oh dear, all we have is honey water out here."

"Sorry," Alex said, pursing his lips. "The axe... it was heavy."

"Well, soon enough you'll be less slender and have

the arms of a man."

"I like my arms, though," Alex mumbled. "Wizards don't need strong arms."

"A wizard, are you now?" Mr. Smith sneered. "How far does a child's imagination go? Men in the real world use their arms. However, you could use your supposed *wizard skills* to speed up your chimney cleaning, which you keep delaying, eh?"

Biting his lip, Alex studied the grass and mud below. There was a good reason to delay sweeping chimneys: he hated it. As much as chimneys benefited the hamlet, they hadn't benefited his health. Luckily, the hamlet only had eight homes and an inn.

"Well, I'm not a real wizard," Alex sighed. "They don't really exist. I got the idea from a really old book I'm reading. He was a hero—the chosen one from a really big wizard school!"

"You could fool me," Mr. Smith laughed. "You see, what you really need is found in all the elders around you."

Alex's lips parted. His eyes rose to meet Mr. Smith's.

Mr. Smith pointed to his thick, round head. "It's knowledge! Knowledge is what's going to move this poor dump forward. Like woodcuttin'! But enough of my rambling! I see you worked hard, but you paid less attention to detail. Detail is what you must pay attention to… detail, detail, detail. As for today's grade, I'll pass a B to your teacher."

Alex's eyes sunk as his shoulders drooped. He had been working so hard for an A in school that year, all because his grandfather said he would turn the radio on less frequently.

"Tell you what," Mr. Smith said as he rubbed his chin. "Smile a bit more, and I might raise your grade to an A minus."

Alex beamed up at Mr. Smith, his smile as wide as he could make it.

"There ya go!" Mr. Smith said with a throaty laugh. "A minus, it is. And be a bit more cheerful, eh?"

Alex nodded. "Yes, sir."

"Good, good," Mr. Smith said. "This is no slave's work or some cruel punishment, I can tell you that. That's one thing you need to understand before leaving this assignment—and a good lesson for them chimneys. We work hard to survive out here in these woods. We set up shop here with our own free, determined hands! No, it's not like the forbidden cities where they have their slaves and electricity do it all for you—that's the real magic used by the rich and their followers. Snap a finger, and anything you want is there—foolishness! When you think about it, what kind of living is that? Where is that old American spirit where you built something with your own hands? I'll tell you what, you can find it right here, and it all starts with woodcuttin'."

Although Alex tried to understand what Mr. Smith said, and tried to pronounce *electricity* with his lips, a rumble in the near distance caught his attention. A wooden cart rolled behind some distant bushes. Its four wooden wheels supported a large, filled corn sack. The driver, who wore an oversized, mucky trench coat and thin black boots, pushed the cart toward the inn.

The ground vibrated—not due to Alex's drumming heart, nor the man's heavy weight, but because a small group of children dashed toward the visitor.

"Trader Tim!" the children cheered.

"Good day, children!" Trader Tim shouted with a hearty laugh. "I must apologize for the long wait! Get your credits because this is the largest collection to date! Hah!"

Alex turned to Mr. Smith, giving in to his need to bounce. "Mr. Smith..."

"Call me Rick," Mr. Smith said with a sigh. "After the whole Helen thing..."

"Rick, can I have my money?"

"That's not a polite way of asking," Mr. Smith said. "What do you say?"

Alex paused, wandering the halls of his memory. "Mr. Smith?"

"No! I mean..." Mr. Smith sighed. "The other word. P..."

Alex's eyes grew wide. "Please! Can I have my money please? Please? Pretty please?"

"There you go!" Mr. Smith laughed, reaching into his pocket. "What was that... three days worth? Here you go."

Alex cupped his hands in front of him. He had dreamed about receiving money of his own for a very long time. His eyes widened as three flat, green-painted rocks fell onto his hands.

"All right," Mr. Smith said. "Now run along with you."

Alex stammered. "Yes, Mr. Smith... Rick! Thank you, sir!"

Alex reached for his cloak, threw it on, and was gone in an instant—like a wizard.

***

Alex rushed into the noisy inn. The building was impressive compared to his home. Its unglazed windows gave an abundance of light, yet the cool air from without battled with the inn's scorching fireplace within. Spider webs wavered along the ceiling's wooden beams. At the far wall, children scrunched in front of a crooked table. They wore ragged tunics, tattered shirts, and cut-off trousers. Adults, who wore their traditional animal hides, quietly came in and smiled warmly at the commotion ahead.

Trader Tim sorted through the bag.

"What's in there?" a boy shouted.

"I need something for my mom's birthday!" exclaimed a young girl.

"Trader Tim will make sure you're triumphant and trim! One moment, and we'll..." The trader paused.

"Oh dear, I can't think of any words that rhyme with *trim*. Nevertheless, I hope you brought your credits today because this was one nightmare of a travel, I'd say! Hah! And... er, not to mention the bloody mess I had to do to get the load of 'dis.'"

Alex's grandfather once bought the radio from a similar traveling trader. The trader claimed voices teleported through the box—what a lie. Although his grandfather's hopefulness may have led it to finally work, there was no proof. To Alex, it was a useless, broken box that went *CRRR!* He wanted to destroy it, and then to jump on it over and over again, just to be certain it had no chance of coming back. Ever since George bought the radio, he treated it like a second grandson; and, quite honestly, Alex felt a little jealous.

"Alex!" Anne shouted near the back of the crowd, both smiling and waving. "Come on!"

Alex dashed toward Anne. The sturdy floorboards felt smooth under his feet, as if the inn had prepared for visitors who never came. The inn was pleasant to Alex, not just because of the lack of splinters, but because it was used for parties, meals, mass, and group games to pass the time during bad weather. Once he caught up with Anne, Alex stood on his toes and peeked above the bobbing heads.

"Where have you been?" Anne asked.

Alex glanced at Anne. "Oh, I was working. I got paid real money today—three green coins!"

"Well done!" Anne said, smiling. "But you know

they're not really coins. They're not like the emperor's coins we learned about in school. We call these 'credits.'"

Alex jerked his head back in dismay. "Credits? So they're not money?"

"They're still money—just different," Anne said. "Do you know how they work?"

Alex shook his head. "I don't remember."

"It's really easy. Three green credits equal one yellow credit, and three yellow credits equal one red credit."

"What goes after red?" Alex asked.

"I'm not really sure," Anne paused. "Purple?"

"Why are there so many different colors?"

"Well, for one, it saves you from carrying a whole bag of rocks on your back!" Anne laughed. "Nobody likes that. So what are you hoping to get?"

"I don't know," Alex said as he stood on his toes again. "I can't see."

"He's really good at lifting items," Anne said. "Well, I guess you already know that—if your memory is working at the moment, unlike your grandfather's!"

"Hey, I resent that!" Alex snarled, then grinned. "I know how to use an axe now! So what do you want to get?"

Anne shrugged. "I don't know. Maybe a radio."

Alex stared coldly at her, only to burst into laughter. "You better not!"

Come to think of it, Alex knew exactly what he

wanted to buy: boots. Traders wore them. They must have brought them from some other world. Sandals were more common for footwear, though scarce. Having sandals either meant you were someone important or an elder, or both. Alex was important— or so he thought with his science skills. Hopefully boots were in the bag, but sandals would do. Cotton would be even better; he needed that the most.

Thinking of cotton, Alex liked his new clothing fashion. He knew he had no choice but to go back to the traditional animal hides if he kept cutting away at the bottom of his shirt for his fire tricks—a bad, yet fun habit.

"Ladies and gentlemen," shouted Trader Tim. "The time has come! I will lift the item, say the price, and whoever shouts first and possesses the credits will be the new owner. Let me hear it! Are you ready?"

Alex cheered with the crowd. Feeling the need to bounce again, but standing near some of the older boys, he pursed his lips and stayed in his place instead.

Alex studied the colored rocks in his right hand. "What do you think three green credits will buy?"

Anne shrugged. "It won't buy a lot. Small things. Remember, three green credits also means you have one yellow."

"How do you remember these things?" Alex asked.

Anne laughed, glancing at Alex. "Some of us pay attention in school!"

Alex took in a deep breath, and muttered, "I try,

but…"

"But you're tired all the time," Anne said with pursed lips.

Alex nodded lightly. He stood on his toes again, staring above the crowd, half in deep thought, half in curiosity.

Trader Tim lifted the first item from the bag. The carved wood had four legs, a back, a small neck, and a long head. Trader Tim spoke with a thunderous voice, "Our first item here is a wooden horse toy for just one green credit – a price I've never offered before! With its small size, you can take it anywhere with you and have the greatest adventures one could ever hope for! Anybody?"

A young girl shouted among the crowd, "I have a green credit!"

Trader Tim pointed to the girl up front. "Sold to the girl with the lovely red rose in her hair!"

Alex's shook his head as his eyes fell. Perhaps three green credits were just three toy horses combined. He shrugged and waited for the next item.

Trader Tim didn't reveal anything too exciting. There was a notebook, a forest-green bracelet Anne bought, a red tunic, used soap, a bottle, and an unknown flat and round object said to be an ancient computer game.

"What is a comp… comp…?" Alex said, trying to pronounce the word.

"I don't know," said Anne, sounding it out with her

lips. "Compoo... I don't know how to pronounce it. He said *game*, though, so I wonder if you throw that round thing like that old Frisbee I bought before."

Alex shrugged. "That might be fun."

Still, there hadn't been anything Alex would like to spend his three precious credits on, especially after his long, tiring work.

"Our next item here..." Trader Tim pulled out something that immediately drew Alex's attention. They looked like Trader Tim's boots but only smaller and white, "... is a used children's pair of levitation-enabled shoes, which allows you to walk on air—parents, be aware! Don't want levitation turned on? Just press the button here on the inward side. These shoes allow you run at a faster speed, keep your feet warm, and keep you better protected. And trust me, my boots are going thin, so these are worth something to you."

Alex thought out loud, "Please say three greens!"

Trader Tim continued, "Given how rare they are, all I'm asking for are two reds!"

"Two reds?" Alex turned to Anne, knowing he was a bit too hopeful. "Do I have enough?"

"No, silly," Anne said. "Two red credits equal six yellows, so... um, eighteen greens."

"Eighteen?" Alex sighed, looking down at his three green credits.

"Sold," shouted Trader Tim, "to the boy with the big belly like myself!"

Alex looked to see who bought the item. It was Oliver. He was a tall, cheeky thirteen-year-old bully. He always enjoyed showing off all his new items. They probably filled his bedroom. Perhaps Oliver slept on them! How he had become so rich was uncertain, though he did hunt in the woods with his father.

Alex had always been surprised that Oliver hunted. He figured that animals would see his big belly from a mile away and storm off. But there he was with widened cheeks as he lifted the shoes over his head. Some clapped in amazement, and others most likely mumbled about revenge plans.

"This is stupid," Alex said with a heavy sigh. "I can't buy anything with three coins—credits, whatever they are. I'll be working the rest of my life for two reds."

"Don't give up! He's not done yet," Anne said. She glanced down at her new bracelet and gave a closed-mouth smile. "Why don't you get something like this? It's pretty, isn't it?"

Alex nodded, rolling his eyes.

The next item made Alex want to drool. Trader Tim lifted what looked like a wizard's wand, except it was half the size, and made of metal. A red button was at the far end.

"Next, we have what looks like a used spring shooter," said Trader Tim. "It consists of a single pipe here. It has a tiny spring inside. When you press the red button here, it shoots out whatever's inside! The options with what you can put inside are limitless! It's so small, I'm only asking for one yellow!"

Alex heard the elders go silent in the back, as if they knew who could find a good use for a mechanical wand like that. At the corner of his eye, Alex saw Mr. Nutter by the wall shaking his head with his index finger wavering back and forth.

"Oh, no," Mrs. Pembleton muttered in the back.

Camping on the cliff tonight just got even more interesting. Alex raised his hand, and shouted, "I'll buy it!"

CHAPTER 4
FIREFLY

"Your father and I used to camp on this hill," said George through the crackling campfire. As he sat on a fallen log, his eyes wandered aimlessly off the cliff. A large darkened forest surrounded the hamlet below.

Alex paid little attention. The fire's warmth made him sleepy in his cozy fur sleeping bag, yet he kept busy preparing his new mechanical wand toy. Licking his lips, Alex stacked the last wet, miniature cotton ball into the thin tube. Alex smiled, knowing he just had to try this out.

George continued, "We would have quality father-son times right here and just talk. Those were the days."

Alex pointed the mechanical wand up toward the sky. He flicked his lighter in front of the tube, pressed the wand's red button, and a miniature cotton ball sprang out! When the cotton ball hit the lighter, it turned into an instant fireball. The fireball flew several feet into the air, streaking toward the sky.

George tilted his head, continuing on with his story. "Or was I just keeping an eye on him as I did community watch?"

Alex's eyes stayed glued to the fireball. George hadn't noticed it. The fireball flew further into the air… and then a slight wind blew it toward George.

"Oh, no," Alex whispered.

The fireball flew directly above George.

"Umm…" Alex quickly hid the mechanical wand in his right pocket.

The fireball fell downward toward George. It hit George's fur pants, setting the left leg aflame.

"Grandpa!" Alex shouted, pointing at the burning pants.

"What!" George yelled, noticing his pants were on fire.

George patted his left leg quickly until the small fire went out. He looked left and right, then upward, and yelled, "Where did that come from?"

Alex gulped. "A firefly?"

"A firefly?" George shouted, and then scratched his head. "I guess that would make sense. But, wait a minute! How can a firefly… When did…"

"I miss Dad," Alex said, quickly changing the subject. "I wish Dad would come back. How come he never visits?"

George straightened his oversized army hat. He kept an eye out for additional fireflies. He glanced at Alex, and said, "You're too young to understand such things."

"But you said you would tell me," Alex protested,

finding himself serious.

George froze with narrowed brows. "I did?"

"Yes!"

"At your age?" George's tongue poked into his left cheek. "Well, perhaps you're ready. Your father and I would view Winter Brooks just over there in the distance. Do you see it?"

Alex squinted his eyes toward the pointed direction. Looking downward made him feel dizzy. In the far distance, countless trees and mountains guarded a well-lit city.

"That's where the empire's regional governor sits. He assists the emperor on local matters," said George. His voice grew sour. "Governor Mallis."

Alex nodded. "Our teacher said we hid from him a long time ago because of our ancient beliefs—that we stand for freedom."

"That's right!" George nodded, his posture straight. "Freedom from tyranny!"

Alex glanced at George. "Tyranny is a bad thing, right?"

"Yes, very much so," George said, tightening his fists. "We're no American slaves to a tyrant."

"Why can't they be friends with us?" Alex asked.

"Now that's a good question," George said. "This used to be a prosperous nation long ago that gave American citizens rights and freedoms, but human nature came in, desiring power after the..."

"Great Civil War?"

"Splendid, my grandson!" George smiled. "That's what we old folks call it, anyway. Long ago it happened, and now it's just a mere traditional name in these parts. While the country fell into madness, someone had to claim leadership."

"Wait," Alex said. "I don't understand."

George looked up to the numerous stars in the sky, perhaps to think—or, Alex thought, to keep a lookout for fireflies. "Try to imagine this: you're playing with your friends on your very own island, but then everyone gets angry at each other."

Alex shrugged. "I don't have many friends."

"Well, say that you do… it makes no difference," George said. "Say that they split up and call each other bad names. Well, you and your friends might not get along for a while. Then imagine it gets much worse—now they're throwing punches, and then there's fire and… well, you get the idea. But then some of your old friends gain allies."

"What are allies?" Alex asked.

"They are groups of people who unite over an agreement or treaty; they help each other out for mutual benefit. In a case like this, those groups make efforts to put the whole island back into order. The more allies you have, the more you're able to gain control of the land. Sometimes the wrong person can come in to take the lead."

"Like Oliver?"

"Sure, it can be anyone. Restoring order might

involve force. You might want to make your old friends follow you... or else!" George leaned in toward Alex with bulging eyes. "Or else!"

Alex lifted his sleeping bag over his mouth and chuckled.

George continued, "Here's the problem with that. Maybe your friend, Oliver, didn't want to restore the land back to how your friends originally found the island, so a new order develops."

"Oh," Alex said, recapping for a moment. "So that's what happened?"

George shrugged. "If my memory is working."

"Well, I don't like Oliver because he's so rich."

"Some people are," George said. "That's another way of splitting the land – by dividing the rich and the poor. Hillcrest Village, one of them eastern towns here in the Olympic Peninsula region, is a good example. We rebellious Americans, whom *they* call savages, are even poorer than the poor, but we have each other. You're lucky to have me."

Alex shrugged.

"Where was I going with all of this?" George asked. "Oh yes, this city that you see ahead of you is where your father went."

Alex squinted his eyes toward the city again. "Why did he move there? It's so small."

"Oh, it's quite big, for sure," said George. "We're looking at it from afar, so it only looks small. As for your father, he would have been allowed to live there if he were accepted. If they didn't accept him, or thought he wasn't being honest, they would pretty much end his... well, I shouldn't go there. Anyway, he got tired of our way of living."

Alex's eyes wandered the countless stars aimlessly. "Maybe he didn't want to clean chimneys anymore like me."

"No, no," George said, shaking his head. "He said

he'd rather live with what *is* than what's *ideal*—like a hope to live for, such as independence and freedom.

"Your mother, Debra," George continued, "held onto you and refused to go with him. She threatened divorce. Some say your father burned the house down out of anger, and I think it was you, but regardless of what happened, your father was kicked out. No one has heard from him since. Seems like life these days, desiring material things over family and values... Back in my day... no, I guess it felt all the same."

Alex rubbed his left fist against his chest. "Dad left because of me?"

"What?" George asked, as if Alex heard him wrong. "No, no. Your mother, on the other hand, felt she made a grave mistake when she demanded him to leave, and so she went off to search for him. She told me to take care of you until she came back. She never returned. And here I am still taking care of you! You're going to be working for me the rest of your life to pay what's due, I hope you know. I intend on being here."

Alex shifted his eyes toward the deep woods. "Maybe the monsters found them."

George scoffed. "There are no real monsters."

"Yes, there are!" Alex shouted. "You said so yourself! Even my teacher..."

"That's all just to scare you," George mumbled.

"What?"

"It's to keep you children from going out there in the deep woods and getting lost—nobody likes that.

Where do you think my wooden statues go? To whom these statues are intended to scare… to make them run back home to mommy and daddy." George's laughter halted. "Maybe I shouldn't have said that."

"I don't believe you," Alex said, looking away. "Then why haven't they come back for me?"

George let out a deep sigh. "Maybe they were captured by the *other* monsters."

Alex tried to control his trembling chin. He rubbed his mechanical wand through his pocket.

Alex's memories of his parents were vague. All he remembered was his mother's comforting smile and his father who taught him some small science tricks, usually something to do with fire. His father said his tricks were part of his job—entertaining people with illusions. Perhaps his father had used an illusion to disappear from his life.

Alex vaguely remembered his parents arguing at night, which would sometimes make him cry. Regardless of why they argued, Alex had always hoped his father would come back to see all the new fire tricks he could do now. Feeling less hopeful, Alex examined the unused cotton in his hands. The faint wind gently brushed some away.

"Do you think they may still be alive?" Alex asked. "Maybe they have been trying to reach us."

George's face lit up. "That's a marvelous thought! What a great second reason to bring up the good ol' radio!"

"Seriously?" Alex squeezed his eyebrows together.

George grabbed the small sack from his side and pulled out the radio. "Let's see what we can find out here, shall we?"

"No!" Alex wanted to plug his ears, but the radio turned on before he could.

CRRR...

"Grandpa, turn it off!" Alex shouted. He was sure the hamlet would wake up any second; the static noise sounded like a rainstorm during a clear evening.

CRRR...

"What?" George shouted.

Alex raised his voice even higher. "Turn it off!"

CRRR...

"What?" George hollered.

A brilliant idea overcame Alex. He shouted, "There's a firefly coming toward you!"

"What?" George shouted louder. "I can't hear you!"

CRRR...

Alex fell on his back as his cheeks burned. He plugged cotton into his ears and shouted, "I'll just plug my ears and go la, la, la!"

The radio *CRRR'ed* on: "*CRRR...* Yes, with the new, sudden rise of... *CRRR...* 'erica... *CRRR...* no one would have ever... *CRRR...* 'ieved... *CRRR...*"

Alex froze; his mouth fell open. His widened eyes turned to his grandfather.

"Did you hear that?" George laughed, slapping his

knee. "And ya'll thought I was mad! Hah!"

CHAPTER 5
THE RADIO'S LAST DAY

Moments later, Alex had his right ear pressed against the warm radio speaker. His wide, unfocused gaze reflected the campfire and his grandfather's pleased smile.

"How can someone's voice teleport into the box?" Alex asked eagerly, turning toward his grandfather. "Is it magic? What is he saying?"

"Shhhh!" George whispered.

The voice continued through the speaker: "*CRRR...* rebellion of the empire's savages... *CRRR...* documents found... *CRRR...* Aydren...*"

Alex's eyebrows rose. "Who's Aydren?"

"Oh, yes, yes," George said, playing with his beard. "That's the emperor's heir... his son—the one who will take over his father's throne one day, if he hasn't already. I remember he was born about your time."

The radio continued, "*CRRR...* hero... *CRRR...* no one knows how long... *CRRR...* outskirts may wish to keep... *CRRR...*"

George narrowed his eyes as he pursed his lips. "Outskirts may wish to keep... what? The outskirts would be us."

CRRR....

George wildly shook the radio a few times fruitlessly, eventually just shaking his head. "This box isn't working so great anymore."

Alex sat up straight, eyes wide with excitement, and said, "Wait! The box never gave a teleporting voice from below. We can hear it up here." His eyes darted around him, finally settling on the ascending hill behind them. "The hill... what if we go even higher?"

"Now, that's my grandson!" George gave a crisp nod. "Come! Help your old grandfather up! These old muscles aren't what they used to be."

Alex scrambled up, took his grandfather's the hands, and pulled him to his feet.

"Just over there!" George said, pointing to an obscure path that led up the hill. "Be careful. Take the radio. I'll be right behind you."

"Really?" Alex asked, narrowing his brows. "You never let me touch the radio."

"Go on," George said, insisting, pressing the radio into Alex's hands.

Alex smiled brightly, and thought, *Should I treat this as an honor?*

Alex took the radio. He had never felt anything like it, and marveled at how smooth it was. Despite the delicacy of the wonder in his grasp, he turned and ran up the gloomy path.

George shouted from below, "Wait for me!"

But Alex sprinted higher and higher, the campfire's

light growing dimmer and dimmer. Each step improved the voice's teleportation, but it also frightened Alex all the more as he climbed higher.

"Just don't look down," Alex warned to himself.

The box teleported a second voice: "*CRRR...* Exactly, I hear what you're saying. The change of powers was just announced a few days ago by Aydren. And with the restoration of America, there's no telling how long the rest of the empire... *CRRR...* comply."

"Grandfather!" Alex shouted, glancing back. "It's better up here!"

"What?" George shouted from below. "Did you just say you could smell my fart from up there? Dear golly!"

"The teleportation!" Alex shouted. "It's better up here!"

From the magical box came another mysterious deep voice.

CRRR...

"Now, how the empire will reform back to its ancient way of life is problematic. Restoring what used to be the United States of America will be a huge effort, if it is even possible. Is it likely politics will follow? Perhaps rebellious leaders will be on the rise? Maybe even war?"

"I wouldn't go that far," said another with a raspy voice, giving in to a nervous laugh. "We don't want to scare anyone on this radio show with speculation."

"Well, all I'm saying is anything is possible," said

the one with the deep voice. "To see the royal family letting go of their positions in order to see this overhaul realized is unbelievable. How do you begin such a task?"

"Well," said the original voice, "it begins with the documents that were found. These documents will give us clues to America's foundation. It was Aydren, the emperor's heir, who found all of the lost documents: the Constitution, The Declaration of Independence, and the Bill of Rights. These ancient documents were thought to be legendary."

With all of his excitement, Alex was a bit confused. It wasn't what he heard on the radio, but rather what he saw in the distance that unsettled him. His eyes squinted. Heavy billows of smoke rose from the north woods. Wanting to get a better glimpse, Alex stepped closer to the hill's edge. He grew nauseous.

"I'm almost there!" George shouted. "Step fifty-three... step fifty-four..."

The radio continued with a new, yet hurried voice: "*CRRR*... there is breaking news that Governor Mallis is trying to keep order in the outer..."

Alex's hands felt lighter than a moment before. The magical voices faded away, as if they were descending a bottomless pit. The ground was missing.

Realizing too late what had happened, Alex crashed hard against the steep hill and rolled down in tremendous pain. He reached for any raised tree root he could find, but missed each one. A thick tree abruptly ended his fall, and the last thing he remembered was a loud thud, and then darkness.

***

Alex woke up with a severe headache. An elder sobbed nearby as a dog howled. Alex opened his heavy eyelids, anxious to see who was crying for him. A small lamp lit the dark room. Brown fur blankets lay over him. His cloak hung on a wooden chair.

Alex found his mourners: it was Grandpa and Max, both shedding tears with great sadness. They weren't facing him; rather, they were facing something broken on the desk that looked all too familiar. His grandfather cried out, "My radio!"

Alex sealed his eyes shut, feeling heat spread over his cheeks. He lifted his arms to cover his ears, but while he did so, a sudden, sharp pain sprang up his left arm. "Ow!"

"My..." George paused, turning around with an open mouth. "Grandson?"

Max, both barking and wagging his tail, ran hurriedly toward the bed, jumped onto it, and licked Alex's face repeatedly.

"Hi to you, too, Max." Alex said, leaning up with his better arm. "What happened?"

George walked toward the bed. "You fell off the cliff—with my radio, I might add. How are you? Are you feeling any pain? I sure hope —"

"I did?" Alex winced as he held his left arm. "My arm... it hurts."

A hefty man with brown-toned skin walked into the room. His black beard was short and untrimmed, and his animal hides had a red tint to them. A warm smile spread across his face as he nodded to both Alex and George.

"Dr. Drew," George said with a sigh of relief.

"How's the boy?" Drew asked.

"He just woke up," George said. "Something about his... um, I have a question. Why don't we have any radio specialists in these parts?"

"Radio specialists? What?" Drew spotted the various radio pieces scattered about the desk. "Oh... If I were you, I'd be more grateful that your grandson is alive."

"I am... I am." George's eyes glanced away. "But my radio..."

Drew faced Alex. "Good to see you, Alex. You're turning more into a man every time I see you—which is about every day in this small hamlet, isn't it? I heard you had quite the fall."

Alex winced. "My left arm... it hurts."

"Here, let me lower the covers," Drew said, doing just that. He head tilted as he pursed his lips. "No bruises. I think it's just sprained. Do you feel pain anywhere else?"

Alex shrugged. "I hurt all over."

"Where do you feel the most pain?" Drew asked.

"My back," Alex winced again. "My legs. And I have a really bad headache."

"I think I would too, if I fell down a steep hill," Drew laughed. "Why don't you just rest for a little while? I'll come by later and check up on you shortly, okay?"

"Okay," Alex said.

Alex wondered why George and Drew froze and stared down on him. He looked down to view the bottom of his shirt. It had been cut in straight lines from all around – cuts that provided the cotton strips for his fireballs. He bit his lips.

"I'll let you both talk," Drew said. "Holler if you need me."

"Yes, thank you," George said, pausing as he played with his beard. "Are you sure you can't do anything for my radio?"

"I'm sorry." Drew patted George's right shoulder. "The radio didn't make it. The best thing for you to do is to move on with your life—and to value those more dearly to you."

George nodded, giving Drew room to leave.

George shrugged at Alex. "No radio specialists. Who would have thought?

"If my memory is working at the moment," he continued, "your shirt looks quite different than it was a few weeks ago. Didn't it used to be longer?"

Alex gulped. "I..."

George cautioned, "You do remember what the

priest taught a week ago."

Alex sighed and nodded slowly. "I used the shirt's cotton for my fireballs so I could be a wizard. I'm sorry. I didn't think anyone would know."

George's eyes widened, trying to hold back either a burst of rage or laughter. "A wizard? There's no such thing as a wizard! Why would you do that?"

Alex tried to muster up an explanation, but he only returned an empty gaze.

"These are all the clothes you have," George said. "Am I right?"

Alex nodded.

"You should know it's not easy to get clothes out here," George said. "If you remember, all you had were those regular animal hides from last year. You said you didn't want to wear what we ancient stick-in-the-muds wear, something about dressing the way all the cool kids dress. It's like the kids plucked out the fur from their hides, making them all these skinny garments!"

"I know," Alex said, lowering his eyes. "I'm still getting use to these new clothes. It's been really useful for my fire tricks, though."

"About that," George paused for a moment, "I don't want you playing with fire ever again. Ever! Why on earth is a child playing with fire in the first place? Where have I been? Oh…" George stared at the broken radio.

George lifted Alex's mechanical wand from the

chair—a toy that begged Alex for more attention. George sat down on the edge of the bed. "I'm assuming this is one of your toys, too? It was found beside you."

"That's my mechanical wand," Alex said. "I just bought it when Trader Tim was here. You press the button to shoot out fireballs. I tried it last night, and..." Alex froze. His eyes locked onto his grandfather's.

George sighed, looking down at the wand. "Firefly."

Alex wondered the fate of his mechanical wand. His grandfather examined it carefully, and he gave it a light squeeze. Moments later, George relaxed his muscles. "You're like your father in so many ways," George sighed, setting the mechanical wand down, still in one piece. "Though you're all I have left of him, which is not a bad thing."

Alex's inquiring eyes glanced down at the unharmed toy and back up again. "So… the radio is no longer a member of the family?"

"No," George replied, shaking his head. "We lived a good three years together. Three years! At my old age, a hobby is what keeps you going—keeps your mind ticking." George sighed. "No. If I learned anything, it's family. I'll pull the blanket up for you. Get some rest, and we'll see how you are for your duties tomorrow morning. Okay?"

"Okay." Alex paused, thinking of some distant reverie. "Grandpa?"

"Yes?" George said as he tucked Alex in.

Alex's downturned face looked out the window beside him. His eyes searched the darkness. "I wish my mom and dad were here right now."

George nodded slowly. "I wish the same. Imagine all the credits your mother is going to give to me for taking care of you! Do you know how many radios that will buy? Goodnight, my grandson."

Alex gulped. "Goodnight."

Alex's heavy eyelids closed. Maybe he could dream

of his parents, or maybe he could dream that the radio
was okay, so his grandfather would be happier.
Instead, he had a dream that would change his world
forever.

CHAPTER 6
DARK RIDERS IN THE NIGHT

"Are you almost done up there?" an adult voice shouted from below.

Alex winced in discomfort as he squinted above. The small opening at the top, which displayed a beautiful view of the pale blue sky, suggested that he was nowhere near the top of the chimney. Instead, he was stuck. His kneecaps were jammed tightly against his chin, and his shins and back pressed firmly against the sides of the narrow shaft. He had become little more than a large amount of soot, covered head to toe in the stuff.

"Yes," Alex called down, sniffling. "Just a few more minutes."

The adult paused, and then asked, "Are you crying up there?"

"No," Alex whimpered. "I'm just cold."

"Ah," the adult said. "Well, when you come down in a few minutes, I'll have some hot soup prepared for you."

"Okay." Alex shook his head as he slowly swallowed the horrid taste in his mouth.

Alex had grown to dislike the thin flues in his

hamlet. When he was younger, climbing up the tiny shafts was no problem. Now nearly eleven years old, it was time to retire. However, quitting would mean that another, younger child would have to perform the vile labor. Postponing meant getting stuck in a flue, and there he was stuck in a flue.

The voice shouted from below again, "I'll see how you're doing in a few minutes."

"Okay," Alex said, biting his lips.

Alex wanted to climb to the top of the flue. The thought of being free and going on an adventure motivated him to finish the job. However, the more he struggled to get free, the tighter he had become.

Above the chimney came a creepy, whiny grunt.

Alex looked up. A goblin with glowing eyes stared down at him. Its eyes narrowed. The goblin started climbing down from the top, sending ash and soot tumbling down onto Alex.

The boy struggled to get free, but his efforts only tightened the chimney's grasp. He looked up again, finding the glowing eyes descending toward him from within the ash clouds.

"Help!" Alex yelled. "Somebody help!"

***

Alex's eyes flung open as he leaned up, panting. His blankets and pillow were soaked in sweat and tears. Having escaped what must have been a nightmare,

Alex said breathlessly, "I'm never climbing chimneys ever again!"

"Somebody help!" he heard from outside, accompanied by trampling feet.

Alex tried to control his breathing. Who was that? He held his breath—nothing.

Wait, there it was again! Then another scream, and another! Alex glanced around the poorly-lit room. George snored on a chair against the wall.

"Grandpa!" Alex yelled. "Grandpa, wake up!"

"I'll buy that radio for five reds!" George shouted happily, as if he was waking up from a delightful dream. "Err, what is it?"

"Do you hear that?" Alex asked.

"Hear what?" George listened harder. "Oh... I do."

Alex gripped his blankets. "What's happening?"

"I don't know," George said, pursing his lips. His voice trailed off as his eyes danced about. He stood promptly, briefly faced the door, and then towered over Alex. He shouted, his tone urgent, "Tell me, what did you hear on the radio when you were up on the hill? Quick!"

"Nothing," Alex stammered with rapid blinks. "Wait! I... I saw smoke rising from the cliff! I'm sorry, I must have forgotten earlier."

"Go on!" George demanded.

"That's all..." Alex tried to think harder. "Oh, and something about the governor..."

"What about the governor?"

"I... I don't remember. Something about keeping order."

George stormed toward the doorway. "Stay here!"

"Grandpa!" Alex shouted. "Don't go!"

"It's those monsters, I tell you!" George yelled, grabbing his army hat.

Max leaped off the bed and raced George down the hallway, toward the front door. Alex was in too much pain to get up and follow.

"Don't leave me!" Alex yelled.

The front door slammed shut.

Are they really monsters from the woods? Alex thought. *Grandpa said they were made up*!

What Alex saw through the window made his jaw drop. Dozens of soldiers in dark uniforms rode into the hamlet upon hovercycles. Their animated belts contained either fire or magic inside. How they managed to do that without hurting themselves was a strange sight to see—it just *had* to be magic.

George shouted from the front door, "Monsters! You're all monsters! Every last one of you!"

In addition to George's yelling and Max's barking outside, several more screams continued to build up around the home. All Alex could do—though he didn't want to—was stay still and listen.

A gravelly male voice shouted from outside, "What have we here?"

"Leave us alone!" a woman cried. "We're just peaceful villagers!"

Another man shouted, "On whose orders do you make this entry?"

"Who else?" the voice replied. "I, Governor Mallis. Do you have more than one authority? Let me tell you, there is only *one* authority—and it is not yours, you savage! Into the inn with you! Every one of you!"

"Monsters!" George yelled. "You're all filthy scum!"

"You too! Take him!" Governor Mallis shouted, and then paused. "Officer Kelly!"

A female's voice replied, "Yes, sir?"

"Search the old man's home and see if anyone else is in there. There cannot be any runaways. Is that clear?"

"Yes," she said. "Is this the last of the settlements? We shouldn't kill too many innocent lives. If Aydren finds out..."

"Officer Kelly," said Governor Mallis as he calmed his voice, "you're a fine soldier. But when I want your opinion, I'll ask for it. As you know, Aydren stepped down from the throne. No one runs this land right now. Savages are a threat, and so they are more expendable to send our message to the rest of the region. We carry on with the plan."

Alex's eyebrows rose.

"Yes, sir!" Officer Kelly responded.

"Good," Governor Mallis said. "Don't forget what fear brings. Go!"

Seconds later, Alex's front door burst open. The

floorboards creaked slowly from the living room to the hallway, raising the hairs on the back of Alex's neck. His heart raced. He kept silent as a mouse.

Footsteps came toward Alex's bedroom. The soldier stepped in, wearing dark leather boots. It is all Alex could see, for he was hiding under the bed. He had no idea how he got under it, but he was somehow in less pain than before.

"It's clear," the officer said. "I'm checking the next room."

"Good," said Governor Mallis through some kind of device, his voice sounding similar to those that were teleported through the radio. "After you've scanned the house, burn it."

Not if I can help it, Alex thought.

With an eruption of pain and several winces, Alex crawled out from under the bed. He stood up and examined the room for his mechanical wand, finding it resting on the bed. He took it. The slender rod still contained a few cotton balls inside.

"I hope this works," Alex whispered.

Leaving his cloak behind, Alex tiptoed down the hallway. He found the soldier searching his grandfather's bedroom. Alex took out his lighter and held it in front of his mechanical wand. With squinting eyes, he pointed it directly at the soldier.

***

Moments later, Alex rushed outside his home. He hardly remembered what had just happened—it was over too quickly. He recalled that his fireball shot out, but missed the soldier, and landed on a bookshelf instead. As the bookshelf burst into flame, he remembered he just held the bedroom door shut while he felt the fire getting warmer. And then he just ran. He looked behind him; his grandfather's bedroom was in flames. To his relief, Alex watched the unharmed soldier escape the burning home in time.

While running away from the soldiers and toward safety, Alex felt that something was wrong. He was the only one running. He stopped, turned around, and faced the hamlet.

Why is everyone being forced into the inn? Alex thought.

All of the villagers—including Alex's grandfather and Anne—were walked by force toward the inn. A few soldiers marched toward Alex's house with bushy sticks in their hands. Their sticks caught the fire Alex started. The soldiers lit up the rest of the buildings, and finally set the inn ablaze.

"No!" Alex cried. "Get out!"

Alex wanted to do something, but there were too many soldiers. Cries and screams rose from within the burning inn.

"Get out!" Alex yelled louder.

Tears streamed down Alex's face. He made out Mr. Nutter's drooped face through the inn's window, staring at the soldiers. He raised his index finger, and he shook it back and forth in sync with his head.

Breathless, Alex collapsed to his knees. He thought maybe, if he acted quickly, he could run to the river with a bucket, fill it with water, and return as a hero. But then a section fell in from the inn's roof, then another, and another, until the whole thing collapsed.

Smoke and flames rose higher, and with it something else that caught Alex off guard.

A dark, evil spirit in a black robe rose above the ashes and blaze. A dark, evil laugh of victory erupted from deep within the hood. Alex caught a glimpse of a face that looked like depictions of Governor Mallis, except with glowing red eyes. The spirit's boney index finger pointed directly at Alex.

I don't think I'm imaging this, Alex thought. *Why does the spirit look like Governor Mallis?*

Was this in Alex's imagination? He only pretended to be a wizard while playing or daydreaming. He just wanted to play, imagining of little fantasy adventures in his own made up worlds. The vicious cloud that bloomed over the inn looked too real. It was every bit as real as the trauma Alex had just witnessed, just as real as the flames and smoke. Alex wanted to get away from the real world and hide in his own imaginary one, but it felt as if both worlds had suddenly collided together.

Governor Mallis shouted from in front the inn, "After him!"

"After him!" the dark spirit echoed.

"Bring the boy to me!" Governor Mallis shouted.

The dark spirit echoed, "Bring the wizard boy to me!"

Wizard? Alex asked himself. *I'm not a wizard.*

The ground rumbled like an earthquake. Muddy hands dug their way through the soil to the surface. Dirt flew aside as scrawny, dwarf-like bodies climbed out. They had pointed ears and noses, sharp teeth, and terrifying claws.

Why do they look so familiar? Alex thought.

The creatures shouted, their cries gravelly and whiney, frightening Alex. One of them, which looked like one of his grandfather's carved goblins, turned and gave him a chilling grin.

Alex took a few steps back, turned, and ran for his life through the woods. He was unsure where he should go, but knew that he had to find a place to hide.

Leaves and twigs crunched behind Alex, growing louder with every stomp.

"Help!" Alex shouted.

Shrieks raged from behind Alex. Some of the goblins had scrambled up into the trees, jumping from one to the next in an effort to catch up to their prey. Panting, Alex pressed on.

Alex darted past several trees. One of the trees seemed to turn to face him as Alex passed it, but he had no time to stop and look at this strange occurrence.

Surely, Alex's imagination must have run wild: the dark lord—whom he named Lord Mallis—and the goblins looked terrifyingly real and vivid, more than he had ever imagined when he played. He ran without bravery, without any further dreams or hopes of becoming a hero; he simply became a victim, a true savage without any home or family to go back to.

Alex had never run so far from his home, but he

had to get away from the goblins. He knew a revenge plan would follow—an adventure he had not planned to take.

But, in these first steps on his grand journey for revenge, Alex tripped and tumbled down another steep hill.

"No! No! No!" Alex shouted as he bounced down the slope. "Not again!"

Alex attempted to catch some friction with the ground, but nothing slowed him down until a large tree—one with enormous closed eyelids—waited for him at the bottom. Alex crashed into it with a loud, painfully familiar thud. His vision went black.

CHAPTER 7
ALONE WITH MONSTERS

Fingerlike shadows of tree branches lay over Alex. They gently swayed left and right until they shuddered, the movement accompanied by a deep, rumbling voice: "This must be the boy."

Oh no, Alex thought, coming round.

Alex had hoped he had escaped from all the monsters last night. After smacking into two trees, he wondered if the voices were in his head. He just wanted to fall back to sleep, but a rough, barky object slowly felt its way up his shirt.

"Cotton," the rumbling voice said again. "This is surely and regrettably our forest burner."

"Forest burner?" Alex thought out loud.

Alex opened his eyes. As his blurry vision cleared, his heart jumped. He blinked his eyes a few times. What he saw above were four curious, eighteen-foot trees, each with bulging eyes that stared down at him.

Blinking more did not help. The tree creatures were still there, just as hideous. Contorted, yellow-brown warts and green moss covered their wooden bodies. Tiny insects crawled across their bark. Two heavy branches extended like arms from either side. Their thick hands made Alex wonder if they could even pick up a fork.

The shortest tree, roughly three feet shorter than the others, had the least amount of bark. His thick hands seemed able to close more than halfway, something the other trees' couldn't. His face resembled a human of about seventeen years old.

These things couldn't have simply been Alex's imagination; they were all too detailed. Alex couldn't have made up details to such an extent; they must truly be right in front of him. Had he hit his head that hard?

Without knowing what else to do, Alex shoved his hand into his pocket.

Alex stammered, "Stay back, or... I'll... I'll shoot!" Alex pulled out his mechanical wand. His trembling hand pointed the wand at the tree monsters. "My grandfather told me about you monsters! I'm not afraid of you!"

The tree monsters looked at each other with widened eyes, only to shrug their shoulders. Taking advantage of their poor reaction, Alex pulled out his American flag lighter. He set in front of the pipe, pressed the wand's button, and a fireball burst out. The fireball flew a few inches until it collapsed to the ground—a dud.

"I think so, too, Trey," said one of the elder trees. "He wouldn't have one of those fireball shooters with him if he weren't our forest burner."

"What?" Alex shouted. "I didn't burn down any

trees!"

"Silence!" another of them ordered. "We know what you did and the cost you had to pay for it. Our sources say you burned your own home down... twice!"

"And another source said you chopped up our tree family for money," Trey said sternly. "What do you have to say for yourself?"

Alex shook his head. "You're not real! Trees don't talk! They don't even have names!"

"Rubbish!" a third shouted. "Don't you recognize our faces?"

Alex stared blankly.

"Your grandfather carved our faces," Trey explained. "He made me uglier than Trent."

"And right he was," said another tree, apparently named Trent.

"Please," Alex begged, "you have to believe me!"

Trent raised his chin. "We were waiting for you to come out here to can hold a trial. Isn't that right, Trewbert?"

Trewbert nodded. "That is so. Let the court begin. All surrounding trees will be our jury."

"Guilty!" Trent blurted.

"We've only begun," said Trewbert. "But yes, yes... I wholeheartedly agree, for he burned us trees and even profited from us! This is most tragic. Therefore, I hereby sentence Alex to shame!"

"Shame!" shouted the trees.

"Forest burner," Trent said, "take your cotton shirt off and burn it before everyone to claim you learned your lesson."

Alex felt his shirt's fabric at the bottom. "It's my only shirt. Honestly, I don't have any more fireballs!"

"Honestly?" Trent shouted. "You have a few more left in the pipe!"

"How can you tell?" Alex asked curiously.

"Enough!" Trent yelled. "Now get to it!"

"I swear I won't do it again!" Alex exclaimed. "Please, I didn't do most of the burning! A dark spirit rose over the inn. He's behind it all! He's the dark lord—Lord Mallis! I saw him! It's all true, even if it doesn't make any sense!"

The elders' mouths grew open.

Trent glanced at Trewbert. "The... da... da... dark lord?"

Trewbert said, "He hasn't been heard from for many, many... I don't know... days? Is that right, Trey?"

"Three days," Trey said.

Trent nodded. "That sounds about right."

"What are you waiting for, Alex?" Trent said.

Alex formed his lips to protest, but then the younger tree stormed in front of him. Each step caused the ground's roots to detach from his feet and reattach as it landed.

That's impossible, Alex thought as his mouth fell open.

The younger tree's voice rumbled the ground. "Stop!"

"Trin," Trent sighed, "My son, I told you that you were only to watch. You are still young and inexperienced. This criminal already faced a valid trial for his grave offenses. It was agreed to sentence him to shame."

"Shame!" the trees shouted again.

Trin shook his head. "What this boy did was terrible, yes, but if he's telling the truth, then the dark lord should be our concern—not this little boy!"

"I don't see your point," Trewbert said.

"I agree," Trey said, nodding his head again.

Trent shook his head at Trin. "I'll take your interruption as unintended counsel. Explain yourself."

"Thank you," said Trin. "Our sources confirmed that the boy just lost everything, and he's dealing with this tragedy in his own strange way. His grandfather is our creator, so shouldn't we grant his grandson some help? Yes?

"Furthermore," Trin continued, "the child seems to be skilled with magic, given his fire tricks. Let me bring him to the wizard school not so far from here. He will be taken care of there, and he will be taught how to use his skill more properly than on us poor trees. Then he can have his revenge."

"That's in Hillcrest Village," said Trent, rubbing his barky chin. "A human settlement."

"Yes," Trin said. "It is, but he would be safer there

than out here."

"That graveyard of trees?" Trewbert said with a sour voice. "You haven't walked that far in years, Trin! You will be exhausted!"

Trey nodded even harder. "I agree!"

Trent nodded. "Trewbert is right."

"The boy can't stay with us," Trin said. "He must be with his own kind."

"I agree!" Trey shouted.

"Trey," Trent said sternly, "you agree with every presented position! A very poor choice for a senator, Trewbert."

Trey nodded all the more. "I agree!"

Alex, still confused out of his mind, listened while the talking trees debated his fate.

"All right," Trent sighed. "But our sources will be keeping a close eye on both of you." Trent turned to Alex. "Go and follow Trin. We'll be watching you, forest burner."

Alex wasn't sure if he should be thankful. "Okay?"

The tree monsters stood there, pity written about their faces. While Alex walked off with Trin, he heard their deep breaths as they mumbled, "Shame... shame... shame."

***

The well-trod forest path led to what Alex hoped to be the village Trin had mentioned. His grandfather said the village's name a few times before, and that it was a half-day's trip. Regardless, the scenery was pleasant with its unending trees and rolling hills. Even the few raindrops splashing against his forehead and cheeks were just as refreshing.

Alex's thin shirt and cut-off trousers rustled with the growing wind. Dark clouds headed his way. Alex's view of the sky was distracted by Trin's wooden bow and quiver carried across his back. The bow reminded Alex of Oliver's, only five times larger. In fact, Trin's bow looked like the same model.

"Shame... shame... shame," Trin mumbled.

Alex raised an eyebrow at Trin. "What? Now you're on their side?"

Trin shrugged. "I'm only saying what's on your mind."

"Right, I'm sure." Alex said, unwilling to admit it. "You know, I never thought I'd be walking with a giant tree by my side."

"We have always been by your side."

"That sounds freaky."

"Freaky as it may be, there hadn't been any reason for us trees to walk," Trin said. "We're the guardians of the forest, stationed right where we're supposed to be. We've kept an especially close eye on you."

Alex rolled his eyes. "Like everyone else."

"Listen," said the talking tree. "Before I forget, I wish to thank you for giving me this first mission, and for giving me the name Trin."

Alex grinned, sinking his brows. "I named you Trin? Your mom and dad did, not me. But how come your face looks so... half human and half tree?"

"We can turn into many forms," Trin said. "We can somewhat imitate a human so you feel more comfortable."

"Comfortable?" Alex said. "You're a giant, walking, talking tree with ants crawling all over you! How old are you?"

"I'm one hundred seven."

"No way!"

"Well," Trin said, "in human standards, my face is about seventeen. The others you saw are about four hundred years old. How many years have you?"

"Ten!"

"Well, you're a young sprout then."

"No I'm not!" Alex shouted. "I'm turning eleven sometime this week. My grandpa knows the... right day..."

Alex's legs grew heavier until he could no longer move. He looked up at Trin inquiringly. His lips trembled as he asked, "Where's Grandpa?"

Trin gave out a deep sigh. He knelt down on one knee, shaking the ground with the weight. "Alex, you wanted to escape from the real world, so I can't tell you where he is. It's better not to know."

A tear rolled down Alex's cheek. "Maybe I can go back. Maybe..."

Trin shook his head. "You left the real world for an

adventure you had always dreamed of! No more work for you!"

"But not like this," Alex sniffed. "If I left the real world, then why am I still in the same forest? Why are some of trees dying? Why is there still evil like Lord Mallis?"

"There are some things your young mind cannot understand right now," Trin said. "Evil will always come lurking to find you, but you can overcome it."

Alex sniffed his nose. Cooler air seeped through his rags.

"And happy birthday to you," Trin said behind a barky smile. "Many don't see being alive as a daily gift. The village is not so far from here. Come."

Alex wiped the tears from his cheeks. With a slight push from the wind at his back, he stepped forward.

***

What had once rested under Alex's aching feet no longer clung to the world. The dirt flew freely from behind with the gentle, cool breeze. Eventually, gravity and increased sheets of rain pulled the dirt back down, restoring what once fled from the world as mud.

Then the waters gathered enough to form puddles, though small enough for Alex to jump over. As the puddles grew larger, he had a harder time. His feet splashed through one puddle after the other.

Water dripped from Alex's hair and streamed down

his sallow cheeks. Surely, his mind was somewhere else. It helped him to forget the rain pounding on his head and shoulders. It helped him to forget the world he once came from. The real world was closing in on him from behind, and he found himself too tired to flee from it.

If Alex was honest, he knew he didn't want to flee from his warm memories. When it would rain like this, he remembered running back home and staying warm by the cozy fireplace. Villagers would meet in the inn to pass time, and Alex would sit near the hearth to listen to fascinating fables and ancient, patriotic American stories.

Alex held his breath a few times as he squinted ahead, but his inquiring gaze would sink again to observe the ground and his mud-spattered legs. He was certain that there wouldn't be a village down this muddy path. Nothing suggested it—absolutely zilch. Alex thought someone should have spent some time putting up road signs, but, then again, he wasn't sure if the villages would want to be found by the dark lord and his monster army. Perhaps Alex walked in the wrong direction, or maybe he listened too much to a walking, talking tree by the name of Trin, who strode nearby, visible in the corner of his right eye. It was nice to have someone there with him… or, rather, some *thing*.

"I hate being poor. I wish I was rich so I could have bought those dumb shoes," Alex mumbled, curling his toes as he walked. "I'm cold. How much further is it to the village?"

"It's near," Trin said with heavier breaths. "It's just down the road a bit more."

"Are you lying?"

"Not any more than you," Trin said. "Do you believe the village is just down the path?"

"Something has to be. A road doesn't just lead to nowhere."

Trin nodded. "Then there must be a village up ahead."

An animal grunted behind them. Startled, Alex and Trin turned around. Through the thick sheets of rain, they found a black horse pulling a large wooden cart. The rider sat underneath the cart's umbrella.

Alex squinted his eyes. "Who is it?"

No response.

"Trin?" Alex turned to face Trin, but he vanished! Alex examined the trees from where he stood, but he didn't see anything that hid or ran away. A walking tree should be easy enough to spot—or at least, he would think. "Trin? Where are you? Trin? Trees, I know you can hear me. Where is Trin? Where is he?"

It was too late for Alex to simply squirrel away like Trin had. The bulky, mud-smeared wheels of the monstrous horse cart rolled forward until it slowed down to a stop beside him. Alex turned to face the cart; his eyes forced upward. An overweight man was sitting there leisurely, in dark clothes, a wide-brimmed hat, and black boots.

"Are you lost, boy?" the man shouted through the deafening rain. "Do you need a ride?"

Alex glanced around for the walking tree again. Only a few trees were unique with that deadly appearance carved into their bark—more than he had previously seen.

The man's face grew bright pink. "Do you need a ride or not, lad?"

Alex couldn't form any words. He would have been fine if the man waved with a polite smile. Instead, Alex gazed past the cart toward the trees on the other end, but there was no giant, tree-bark rescuer.

"I'm asking too many questions. I understand," said the man. "My name is Daryl, a traveling trader and business man in these parts. I have to deliver these bags you see in the back. Don't see them? No? Then you might be a small, stranded child in the deep woods! You're probably dazed with all that chimney soot plastered on your skin, so I'll ask one more time, and then I'm off, okay? Do you need a ride?"

Alex's eyes finally locked onto the cart. He focused on the cloth umbrella above the front. He rubbed his hands. "To where?"

"To the village just down the path, of course," said Daryl. "Can I offer a ride? You look awfully soaked, and this blasted rain is surely no good for you!"

"But I have a friend…"

"You have a friend?" Daryl looked in both directions. "I'm afraid it's just you out here, kid."

Alex gave one last look for Trin. He had no idea where he may have gone. If what the trees said was true, then they would know where he was at all times. Maybe they could tell Trin where he went, in case Trin had stepped away to use the bathroom—what an odd time, though.

"So what's it going to be?" Daryl asked.

Alex lifted his eyes. He never rode with a stranger before, and he felt it was a bad idea. His eyes locked onto the cart's umbrella. With a shiver, he looked at the stranger with pursed lips. He lowered his eyes and nodded.

"Then come on and climb up the ladder," said Daryl. "We have a little bit of daylight left for us. It's best not to waste it."

Feeling he may regret this, Alex grabbed the ladder to the cart and climbed his way in. He immediately enjoyed the umbrella above him. The cart's wheels started to roll forward. If Alex was going where he thought he was going, he was finally off to the wizard school. Without Trin's guidance, though, Alex hoped he was going to the right village—if there was one at all.

CHAPTER 8
THE ARRIVAL

The horse cart's wheels rumbled along the forest path. Alex gripped onto the seat's edge. After a few jerks left and right, the cart's swaying lessened. Sighing with relief, Alex felt the wheels roll onto a smoother part of the path. He resumed his study of the rider seated beside him.

"You know," said Daryl as he glanced at Alex, "if you keep staring at me like that, I might have to tie you to the horse up front, and I'm telling you she's no friend! I learned that the hard way, and I'm still trying to recover. What you see below me is of no mistake."

Alex glanced downward. The man was sitting on a pillow. Alex tried to cover his obvious smile.

"You think that's funny, boy?" the man asked in a serious tone, then with a closed-mouth smile. "Well, that makes two of us. What's your name, boy?"

Uncertain if he should respond, Alex gazed toward the trees again. The rain had settled. He kept one of the cart's blankets wrapped around him for warmth and security. He could use his talking tree for comfort.

Alex caught Daryl's heightened eyebrows. Daryl's free hand reached for an open corn sack below. Alex's muscles tightened, his posture tensed. He pushed himself away, watching Daryl pull out something out from the sack.

A pear?

Well, a pear was less scary than what Alex thought would come out—perhaps a large knife. However, a pear was an acceptable alternative. As Alex stared at it, he couldn't remember the last time he'd eaten. His stomach stirred in great hunger, growling at him. He slowly licked his lips.

"Tell you what," Daryl said. "I'll give you food in exchange for answering a question of mine. How's that? Does that sound like a good deal?"

Alex didn't care what the terms were—he nodded. Daryl lightly tossed the pear to Alex. Alex chomped it down quickly.

"And..." Daryl said, waving his hand.

"Oh, sorry," Alex said with his mouth full. "Alex."

"The young lad speaks!" Daryl said with a smile. "And where are your parents, Alex?"

Alex frowned at the man.

"Oh!" Daryl laughed, glancing at the sack. "How forgetful of me."

Daryl dipped his hand into the sack again. He pulled out a red, delicious-looking apple. He lightly tossed it to Alex.

"I don't have parents, well... anymore," Alex said, and then studied the man again. "Are you real?"

Daryl laughed. "What makes you say that? My large

belly you see here is just as real, as you are! Hah! Coming to the good ol' village to make your fortune, eh?"

Alex looked at Daryl inquiringly.

Daryl explained, "To make money, of course!"

"Oh," Alex smirked. "I'm on a quest to find the wizard school, so I can get revenge."

"A wizard school?"

"Yes," Alex said with a lowering brow. "It's there."

"I didn't say it wasn't," Daryl said, snorting. "That village has its own belly of secrets, I kid you not. Each person has at least three secrets there, so goes the old saying. In fact, just to share one of mine, I'm the master wizard!"

Alex's eyes lit up. "Really?"

"No, bad joke," said Daryl. "Just an old man doing business, I'm afraid, though I'm sure having a magical wand would move things a little faster around here. Maybe you can be my partner when you get your wand."

Alex's body perked up. "What do you do?"

"Well, for one, I look for items, and then I sell them—all to make money, of course. It doesn't matter what they'd be."

"Oh," Alex said, gripping onto his blanket.

Selling came in two ways in the forest. One way was what Trader Tim did, selling merchandise from one village to another. Another method—influenced by the empire—was selling slaves. Slave traders visit hamlets and villages to auction off new slaves of all shapes and sizes. The slave would become property, and then he or she had to follow the master around all day. Alex didn't understand slaves much. He never knew who they were or where they came from. Alex's hamlet did not welcome such traders, and they told them to keep on walking.

"Do you know Trader Tim?" Alex asked.

"Trader Tim?" Daryl asked. "Oh, yes, I do recall. Is he still making a living by robbing and trading?"

Alex stared at him, dazed. "He wouldn't rob from people."

"Not people. Their *houses*, you see? Totally different things."

"They're not totally different... He's a nice person!" Alex raised his chin. "He wouldn't rob. How do you know him?"

"Him and I... we go..." Daryl trailed off. His eyes stared ahead of them. "Well, look at that!"

Alex stared the direction of Daryl's eyes. Just down the lush tree hills, a huge village sprang into sight.

Alex leaned in. "Is that it?"

Daryl nodded. "It is!"

The sight made Alex breathless. He had never seen a village of such great size before. The village had two distinct sections: The first half was poor, filthy, and made of wood; the second half was made of stone, and was cleaner. A wall made of stone surrounded the village, with gates on each side. Alex guessed there were at least a hundred homes, and many shops. Their roofs were at different angles, and they even had chimneys! It looked beautiful, like a painting on a canvas, untouched from the old world he once knew.

Daryl cleared his throat. "Now, once we get to the security gate, remember to stretch out your right arm."

"What?" Alex raised a brow at Daryl. "Why?"

"To have it scanned, of course! Are you familiar with this village?"

"No."

"Well," Daryl said, "this use to be a savage village, but given how large and active it had become, the empire gained control of it. It's kind of a way to remind the American savages on who is in charge. I don't blame the idea. The savages need a reminder from time to time. The savages' only options were slavery, sport, and to affirm allegiance with the empire. But, since the entire land is the empire, I suppose it's kind of a mercy letting them live."

Alex shuffled in his seat. "I..."

Daryl stared at him. "What?"

"I can't go in," Alex stammered. "We're Americans. We're against the empire!"

"What?" Daryl halted the cart abruptly. "You're telling me you're a savage?"

"I have to go," Alex said, undoing the blanket.

Daryl grabbed Alex's arm firmly.

"Leave me alone!" Alex shouted.

"Alex, wait!" Daryl shouted. "Calm down! I said

calm down. Listen: just like Trader Tim, I sell goods to savages all the time—yes, even to you American savages. So, I'm no enemy to you. I won't turn you in. Now, I'm guessing you're an orphan just by looking at your filthy state—it looked like the forest itself jumped you."

It did, Alex thought.

"You said you're looking for the supposed wizard school, right?" Daryl asked.

Alex nodded.

"Good," said Daryl. "I think you're totally out of your mind, but at the same time, you can't just live out here in the woods and expect to live without any parents or what not. What would you eat the next day? What would you do if a bear jumped out of the bushes and had you for supper? Do you have answers for these things?"

Alex parted his mouth, closed it, and shook his head.

"You have no one to go back to, I assume?" Daryl asked.

Alex lowered his eyes and shook his head.

"Here," Daryl said, sighing. "Let me do the talking. I'll explain I bought you as a slave, thanks to evil spirits."

Alex glared at Daryl. He wanted no part in being a slave and following someone around all day!

"No worries," Daryl said, smiling. "It's not true, right?"

Alex relaxed his stiffened shoulders and nodded.

"Then you have nothing to worry about," Daryl said, releasing Alex's arm.

Alex did have something to worry about; it only grew in size as they approached the village's security gate. Scrunching downward, Alex hid terribly. Any Empire settlement was a forbidden place!

"Halt!" a soldier shouted.

The soldier's shaved brown hair caught Alex's eyes. The hair looked silly, as short as that. He could never see himself with such a foreign haircut. The black uniform was also very tight against the soldier's body. No one dressed like that!

Daryl slowed the cart down to a stop. "Relax, Alex."

The soldier walked toward Daryl's side, eying on the two in the cart until he closed in on the big man. "Right arm, please."

Daryl pointed his right arm toward the soldier. The soldier moved a long metal device toward Daryl's arm, and a red scanner lit up at the very top. It gave a beep and a green flash.

"State your purpose here," said the soldier.

"For one, I live here," said Daryl. "My purpose is to eat, drink, sleep, and find myself a lady, and not one of them savage slaves, I tell you what."

Alex watched the soldier smirk with a slight nod, but then he froze as their eyes met.

"Who's the boy?" The soldier asked.

"His name's Alex, a savage slave I just bought with great disappointment," Daryl said, shaking his head. "He's of no use to me, so I'm freeing him as an empire citizen, as law, and then I'm throwing him into the orphanage."

Alex faintly shook his head at Daryl with widened eyes. Daryl's stern eyes returned to him.

The soldier pursed his lips. "What made the slave of no use?"

"He does nothing he's told," Daryl said, glaring at Alex. "When I slap him around it doesn't help him any better, either. To be honest, I think I'm just getting too old. There's no energy left in it for me. I'd rather hack at a pig all day in the market than have this slave around. On second thought, I'd trade him for a pig. Even better, I'd give him away *with* a pig!"

"How long have you owned him?" the soldier asked.

"I just bought him," Daryl said, and then he bit his lip.

The soldier smirked and leaned in closer. "Don't you think you want to give him more time?"

"More time?" Daryl asked. "Listen, I know slaves, and I'm telling you this one is no good. Besides, to be honest, I bought him as a favor—something I honestly, deeply, and utterly regret. He's no good! I hope the orphanage may teach him some good manners, but it might take three of them to finally get through to him. If you keep asking questions, I might have to say he's yours!"

The officer gave a short laugh. "I think I'll pass. Officer Jack, scan the boy's arm on your end."

"Will do," another soldier said, as he walked toward Alex.

Daryl scoffed. "You can scan his arm all you want, but it won't do you any good either. There's nothing there. That's why you don't deal with them savage kinds. They run wild without a cause to their existence. In fact, I don't think they even have a s—"

"Daryl," said the soldier.

Daryl turned promptly. "Yes?"

The soldier leaned in, and said, "Zip it."

Daryl lowered his eyes. "Yes, sir."

Alex tried resisting, but Officer Jack seized his right arm. He watched the machine approach his arm. The machine gave no beep or green light.

"No chip here," Officer Jack said.

Daryl rolled his eyes.

"Daryl," Officer Jack said, "He is a slave of yours, correct?"

"Yes," said Daryl. "Again, I'm kicking him into the orphanage, and I do mean literally kicking him in there."

"Then we'll have to tag him," Officer Jack said as he fumbled with the machine.

Officer Jack asked Alex, "What is your full name?"

"Alex Waycrest," Alex said.

"Age?"

"Eleven, I think," Alex replied.

"You think?" The officer asked. "When is your birthday?"

"Um," Alex said as his eyes veered upward. "April 7, 2881."

"So, you're eleven today," the soldier said. "Happy birthday."

Alex tried to hide a pleased smile, but he wished he could celebrate it with his family. It also meant another year had gone by without seeing his parents. Quite honestly, he didn't know what to feel, or how wide he should smile.

"Hometown?" the officer asked.

When Alex didn't answer right away, the soldier caught his attention. "Alex!"

"Oh," Alex said, lost in thought. "Oakville."

"Okay," Officer Jack said, typing in the last item. "Here we go: there's an orphanage on Pine Street with an available bed."

"What?" Alex said, trying to get his arm back. "No!"

"Alex!" Daryl said. "Don't worry about it. It's just an orphanage. Tagging your arm is a small price to pay for a wonderful world full of one possibility— whatever they assign you to do! Life made simple, eh? No longer dreaming what could be—what a bunch of wasted years. Officer, what is he to be?"

Officer Jack glanced up. "An orphan until an adult citizen at twelve years old, and then off to cleaning services at Bellbrick's Cleaners."

"Oh, splendid!" Daryl said, patting Alex with a wide smile. "Now that's a promising future!"

Tears formed as Alex watched the scanner move closer to his right arm.

"Here's your birthday gift," the soldier said.

A sharp needle injected something into his arm. Alex yelped, and then massaged his painful arm.

Officer Jack nodded. "You're clear to go."

Daryl looked at Alex with a smile. "See, that wasn't so bad, eh?"

"Let them through," said Officer Jack. "On your way."

Daryl turned to Alex, and said with a warm smile, "Welcome to Hillcrest Village."

Chains rolled a heavy gate upward. Once it was high enough, Daryl signaled the horse to walk forward. Alex's future was right through the gate, and it scared him badly.

"You put on a good show over there," Daryl said. "That struggle you pulled off was fine acting."

"I wasn't acting!" Alex yelled.

"All part of the show," Daryl said.

"What's a show?"

"You know, what you see on TV, and..." Daryl met Alex's confused eyes. "Never mind."

Alex stared at his arm again. "What did they put into me?"

"They put in a computer chip that states your role,

tracks your whereabouts, and stores your history," Daryl said. "No worries. Everyone has them. It's just so they can identify who you are, and a few hundred other things. Obey the law, and you'll be fine."

Alex couldn't believe what had just happened. Was he no longer an American? His thoughts vanished when they crossed the security gate. What he saw in front of him was amazing.

A wooden sign read Main Street. Wooden buildings extended, all the way up to four stories tall. Villagers walked up and down the cobbled sidewalks, each going about their own business. The majority had their own pair of shoes and boots, and they wore more layers of clothes than Alex had ever seen on one person.

When there was a traffic opening, some villagers dared to cross the road. Several horse carts rode down the muddy, stone-shod street. The richer carts had transparent, green-bordered rectangles that floated in the air in front of the rider. Teleported faces, similar to the voices that came from Grandfather's radio, talked as they hovered in the air. It was amazing.

Among the people, new smells captured Alex's attention. Local food shops had fresh bread, meats, fish, and other goods.

To Alex's surprise, the horse cart pulled over to the side of the road. Wondering why they had stopped, Alex looked up at Daryl. It seemed as if Daryl had second thoughts for a moment, but then the man turned and tipped his hat.

"Well, this is where I leave you," Daryl said. "I think two yellows is a fair price."

"For what?"

"For the ride, of course," said Daryl. "And for all the lying that should have gotten us killed."

Alex pursed his lips. "I don't have any credits."

Daryl tilted his head with a shrug. "Well, I guess I

should have assumed that given your filthy clothes, soot, and all. As a tip, you'll really want some shoes here, though you lower class folks don't always have much of a choice. Over here—although I'm sure it's more natural being barefoot where you come from— the village associates shoeless people with either being utterly poor or a slave."

Alex's mouth fell open. "Why?"

"Social influences from Winter Brooks, I assume," Daryl said.

"Oh."

Daryl continued, "A benefit of the orphanage is that they may be able to help you with clothes and shoes, if you choose to go there after hunting for your wizard school. Walk down this street here. Then take a right on Brimstone Avenue, and then left on Pine Street. Now off you go."

Alex wanted to pinch himself hard to see if he heard Daryl right. As he unwrapped the blanket, he felt cooler. He went for the ladder, and he carefully climbed down the cart.

After jumping to the ground, Alex didn't like what he just stepped into—something squishy and muddy, like the rest of the street. He could only guess what half of the crud was, with all the trotting horses.

Alex looked up at Daryl, and asked, "Can I stay with you?"

"Oh, no," Daryl said, shaking his head. "You wouldn't want to stay with me unless you had no other choice. I'd hate to see you end up there."

"But you know Trader Tim," Alex complained.

"No, boy," Daryl said firmly. "I must get on to my duties, and you must get on to yours. Maybe we will cross paths again one day. Remember, it's Pine Street for the orphanage. And best of luck finding that wizard school! It could be anywhere! And if you find a magic wand, try to find me because I might need one eventually, oh dear!"

"Wait!" Alex shouted.

Daryl began to ride off. Huge wheels and monstrous horses moved quickly, and Alex had a hard time to catch up to Daryl. The cart faded away, until it became anonymous with the other carts, and then it was gone.

CHAPTER 9
THE SEARCH FOR THE WIZARD SCHOOL

"Out of the way!" a voice thundered.

A horse cart slammed against Alex's left side. Alex spun and twisted until he fell facedown onto the street's awaiting mud.

At least the mud gave a softer landing, Alex thought.

Leaning up, Alex found his clothes filthy and smudged with green and brown crud. The smell was horrid! Was it really mud? Luckily, his face had avoided most of the contact with the stuff.

Another horse cart scurried his way.

"Hey!" the rider yelled. "Watch out!"

Daunting wheels expanded as they rolled toward Alex. With widened eyes, he crawled through the slimy sludge. He jumped, his knees aching, toward the cobbled sidewalk.

Alex turned, seeing enormous muddy wheels roll past him.

The rider raised a fist. "Are you mad? Stay off the street!"

Alex was sure the rider didn't see his trembling nod. He couldn't believe how far he had walked into the road. He had attempted to follow Daryl's cart, but he had hoped the rest of the carts were just a part of his imagination. The cart was real, and the pain was real. Thus, the horse carts and this village surely had to be real, too.

It must have been a joke when Daryl left Alex there. Perhaps he should just sit there and wait for Daryl's return, but for some reason he doubted it was a good idea.

Glancing to his left, Alex's lifted his blushing face. An older man, who wore a top hat and a ripped trench coat, averted his gaze as he sauntered by.

A bearded man in rags came into view. He shook his head and muttered something Alex couldn't understand.

Maybe the walking, talking trees had successfully condemned Alex to shame, and perhaps he felt their condemnation, and even smelled it. Tears streamed down his face. He pressed his knees against his chest, lowered his head, and sobbed.

"Boy," an adult said from behind him. "I saw you on the road, and I..."

"Leave me alone!" Alex cried.

Alex wiped his tears, smearing the green and brown crud from his hands onto his cheeks—he regretted that decision. While rubbing off what he could, Alex only smeared it in some more. A greater stench overcame him. To close his eyes and imagine being somewhere else was his only escape from the noisy traffic, villagers, and the soft jingle that dropped to the ground beside him.

Alex wished he were back in the woods where it was peaceful and quiet. Thinking of that, he knew this was all Trin's fault for leaving him behind. As he thought about Trin, he turned around to see who was behind him, but only found a young man in a trench coat walking away. Something caught his attention at his side. He spotted a small sack tied with a string.

Alex looked up to find whoever had left it for him, but the person was long lost in the crowd. Though disappointed, his eyes locked onto the mysterious sack again. He undid the string and gave a peek inside. His mouth parted. Inside were several green credits!

Alex poured the credits onto his left hand. There were six greens! That's double what he had made just a few days ago!

"Two yellows." His eyes grew wider as he smiled. "That's almost a red!"

Alex remembered two yellows equal six greens, all thanks to Anne who... a deep sigh overcame him. He missed her. Did she die in the fire, too? He remembered Anne was heading toward the inn last night—never mind that. He was certain she was okay. In fact, the tree people had likely saved everyone just in time, probably before they condemned him to shame. Then, when Anne was free, she may have been free from her daily work to study magic. He nodded, biting his lip.

Still, Alex treasured the moment while he held the credits. Everyone else just stared at him as they walked by, as if he was too young to be a homeless beggar. But no matter—he was rich now, or so he thought. Alex secured the money tightly in his hands. He put the credits back into the sack and tightened it with the string. He rubbed his stomach, smelling food from a nearby bakery shop.

"I can't believe you did that!" a young child said from behind.

Did what? Alex wondered.

Too curious, Alex turned quickly. An olive-skinned boy his age stood from behind. His thick black hair fell below his ears, which covered most of his round cheeks and a light bruise near his left ear. Although he had no footwear, he seemed quite warm regardless of how poor and filthy he looked. The boy wore an oversized, dirty-green sweater and dark cut-off trousers that went below the knees. A red scarf and old-fashioned cap kept his neck and head warm.

"Really, I can't believe you went all the way to get that money," the boy said. "That was so cool! Mr. Ratzel will give you something extra tonight, no doubt—food, most likely. He always rewards the bravest, and you know how little he gives when you don't turn up well."

Despite the filthy appearance, Alex stood up and squinted at the odd boy. "Who is Mr. Ratzel?"

"Oh, exactly!" The boy gave a knowing nod. "I guess you're new. When people ask whom do you work for, you want to deny it. Like, *who is Mr. Ratzel? I have no idea who Mr. Ratzel is!* You see, like that! That way the villagers won't know, and Mr. Ratzel won't kick you out like all those orphanages do. But, wow! Just by looking at you, I bet he'll give you lots of food tonight. You see, the other kids don't want to get messy, unlike you and me, and so they often end up short."

"Short of what?"

"Credits!" the boy smiled. "Mr. Ratzel doesn't like that type of laziness when begging, and you don't want to be on his bad side because... well, trust me. So, what is your name?"

Alex stammered, "Alex."

"I'm Antonio," the boy said with a closed-mouth smile. "You see, I come from Italy, but you can call me Anthony if you want."

Antonio continued, "How come I've never seen you before? How much money did you make for Mr. Ratzel?"

Oh, was Alex beginning to think straight at that moment. He closed his mouth and grasped the coin sack tighter. He wasn't going to give his money to *anyone*, especially to a man he'd never met.

"They're *mine*!" Alex yelled, stuffing the coin sack

into his half-ripped pocket. "I have to go. I don't know who Mr. Ratzel is."

"No, really," Antonio said, as he took a few steps closer. "You can admit his name because I know him, too! And you shouldn't hide that money from Mr. Ratzel. He'll get very angry."

"Then let him be angry because I don't know who he is! I don't know anybody! And I don't want to know *you*!"

Actually, Alex did want to know some people here, but he knew better than to talk to a child beggar. He just wanted to run off and find the wizard school—it was around here somewhere. He hoped so, anyway.

Antonio shook his head slowly. "I don't think I like you."

"Then leave!" Alex yelled.

"Don't mind if I do!"

Antonio easily snatched the coin sack from Alex's pocket. He ran down the sidewalk laughing.

"Give it back!" Alex shouted.

Alex chased Antonio, passing several food shops, bumping into several shoulders, and wincing at every curved stone below. Eating would have been an option by now if he just held onto his credits, and thinking about that made him even angrier. He saw Antonio turn the corner and run into some thin, dark alley that read Mudbrick Avenue.

Alex slowed down to a stop as he breathed deeply. The chase was no use. Wherever the child beggar was, he was gone. There were some strange faces along the alley's stone walls though, and the sunset didn't give enough light to show who they were. One of them looked taller, with red eyes, but after a second glance, the eyes were gone. Alex gulped, took a few steps back, and fled back to Main Street.

***

Alex brushed through an endless crowd of strangers. Their eyes focused on wherever they were going, unable to stop and say hello, or show any kindness. They were nothing like the people back home.

Alex wondered if he was on Main Street, but nothing confirmed it. The cobbled sidewalk was his only sense of direction. Looking down, Alex carefully guided his footsteps among a plethora of used shoes and sandals. People stepped on his feet many times accidentally. For what it was worth, he got a good idea of what was on the shoe market. Most of the shoes, often black or brown, went up the ankles a few inches.

Bumping against shoulders grew frequent. Alex didn't mind it as much. Some shouted to watch where he was going, and others just didn't seem to care. Alex wouldn't respond back; he had a feeling it was best to keep silent, being a clumsy newcomer.

Something caught Alex's nose. He sniffed his way toward a bakery shop against the sidewalk. The bread on display made his mouth water. A large brown loaf caught his attention.

"Don't even think about it!" the shopkeeper shouted. Her long gray dress and matching curly hair was just as appalling as her ill personality. "I know how ya street kids think. Thinkin' you can take anything that pleases ya. Off with ya!"

Alex scanned the shopkeeper's irritated face; she was about to explode if he continued to mess with her—it could be fun to find out. However, he simply lowered his eyes and dragged himself away. He didn't want to be a bother to anyone, but he wouldn't mind if another generous person came along. They seemed so few, and he wanted to be nicer next time. However, if these shop people were treating him like a beggar, then perhaps he was one.

***

The sun began to set an hour later. Alex walked on the sidewalk. He crossed his arms against a short breeze.

A freckled woman walked along the sidewalk and headed for Alex.

"Excuse me?" Alex asked.

The woman's nose tilted high in the air. Alex followed her straight eyes as she passed by.

Another disheveled man in a tattered brown suit headed his direction.

"Excuse me..." Alex said, though the man paid no attention. "Please, I'm not a beggar! I'm not asking for credits!"

The man raised a flat hand as he walked on.

A group of females walked by in long, sleeveless tunics. Alex walked toward them.

"Please," Alex begged, "can you tell me where the wizard school is?"

"Wizard school?" The women just laughed as they walked onward, talking amongst themselves. "Wouldn't that be fun? I want to go there!"

How secret is this school? Alex thought.

Another man in rags and sandals walked close by.

"Excuse me," Alex said. "Do you know where the wizard school is?"

"Wizard school?" the man asked, laughing. "What are they feeding street children these days?"

Sighing heavily, Alex felt his rumbling stomach. He pursed his lips. His nose led him to another bakery nearby. He walked into the shop and stared at the bread selection.

"I'll be right with you in one second!" the shop owner said to Alex.

As the shop owner talked with another customer, Alex eyes danced between the bread and the shop owner. He was fixated on a white, fluffy bread loaf. When the shop owner looked away, Alex reached for the bread.

"Thief!" A customer shouted.

"I'm just hungry!" Alex stammered.

"Guards!" the shop owner yelled.

Clutching the bread, Alex turned and stormed down the sidewalk.

"Stop!" a guard shouted.

Alex ran as fast as he could, turning at every corner he saw, breathless as he bumped into many shoulders. Nothing around him looked familiar. Maybe it was to his advantage. He turned at another corner.

Alex smashed into someone who wore a black robe. He fell, and his bread escaped his grasp as it fell to the sidewalk. Fearing he had run into a guard, Alex looked upward. A black hood disguised the person's face.

"I'm sorry," Alex stuttered. He crawled backward as the person faced him. "I..."

Alex's throat locked. Underneath the hood was a girl that mesmerized his eyes. She looked like someone he knew from before—a friend, a longtime companion, and the second greatest and bravest wizard of them all—it was Anne.

The girl's face was exact. She was just as tall, and looked about a year older than him. Alex couldn't see her hair from under the hood, but he was convinced in his mind. Nothing made sense about it. Was he imagining her, too?

"Are you okay?" the girl asked.

Alex nodded, unable to speak.

"Stand up," she said.

Alex stood slowly, unable to look away from the girl's eyes.

"Why do you look troubled? And why are you looking at me like that?" The girl leaned in with narrowed eyes. "What is it?"

Alex tried to catch his breath. "Anne?"

She tilted her head. "Who's Anne?"

Alex was at a loss for words. How can that be? He knew her. Whether she was real or just part of his imagination too, he did not know. She never had such a robe before, and she seemed somewhat more grown up with it on. Regardless, she would be a useful companion.

"Stop messing around," Alex said, glancing behind him. "I'm in trouble. I came to find the wizards' school, and now I'm being..."

The girl stared down at the bread. "You stole it."

Alex swiped the bread off the ground and held it close to him. "I'm hungry.

"Please," he continued. "I must find the wizard school... I traveled a long way. I lost my family. I lost my home. Now I'm... I'm a..." He stared down at the stolen bread and sighed.

The girl hesitated as she pursed her lips.

Alex had to convince her somehow. He looked up at her, and said, "I have a skill with magic."

The girl snorted, and asked, "You can do magic?"

Alex nodded his head. "Please, you must help me. Do you know where the wizard school is?"

The girl hesitated some more, her eyes wavering around, uncertain. The girl glanced around them, and then she looked back to Alex with pursed lips.

She nodded.

CHAPTER 10
THE SEARCH FOR THE WIZARD SCHOOL

While eating the stolen bread, Alex watched the cobbled sidewalk as he walked. He followed the girl's black robe and leather sandals just ahead of his dangling hair.

After the final swallow, Alex paced to the hooded girl along the side. The girl caught his study of her.

"What?" the girl asked.

"If you're not Anne, then who are you?" Alex asked.

A sense of wariness came about her. "It's better that I don't say my name."

"Why?" Alex asked. "Why is it so hard to admit you're Anne? Be brave again! No one else is listening. Are you sure you're not Anne? You sure look like her."

She shook her head and looked forward again. "No, my name is still not Anne."

"What is it then?" Alex asked.

The girl scoffed. "Fine. My name is Kyra. Please keep that to yourself."

Alex slumped slightly. "That's nice… for a fake

name!"

"It's not fake! I've grown to be as fearful as you, so I don't see why it matters. Weren't you just running from the guards? You might want to change your name to be safe. Who is this girl named Anne anyway?"

Alex sighed. "A friend from home. She... Are you really a wizard?"

"Why do you say that?" Kyra asked.

Alex shrugged. "Well, you have a black robe on. All wizards wear black robes, so you must be a wizard."

"Where does it say that in the rulebook?" Kyra said. "Look, I'll show you where the wizard school was, and then I'm heading off. It's not safe out here." Kyra pointed to her left. "The wizards' school is at the edge of the city in this part, where it extends into a small part of the forest. It's right there to your left."

Filled with excitement, Alex quickly looked to his left. He spotted a wooden entrance gate. A burnt road sign hung loose. He tried to read the sign, which wobbled slightly with the wind.

It read *Wizards' Road*.

Alex tried glancing between the living and dead trees. The school was out of sight. Alex leaned in toward the gate. He knew he had come a long way to find this very place. His smile grew while Kyra turned pale.

"This is it?" Alex said.

Kyra shook her head. "This *was* it."

Alex walked toward the damaged gate. "What happened?"

"It was…" Kyra trailed off. "Seriously, we need to turn back! I'm not kidding!"

Alex shrugged it off. "Well, apparently I'm braver than you again. Watch!"

Alex jumped past the border the gate once protected.

"I crossed it!" Alex said. "Nothing happened! Now you can, too."

"Alex!" Kyra shouted. "You can't go in there!"

"Says who?" Alex asked. "I just want to take a look! What's wrong with you? Come on, unless you're not brave enough!"

Kyra rolled her eyes and stormed toward the gate. Alex couldn't believe how long the road was! It was a dirt path that led to some kind of structure ahead. He could tell Kyra longed to see it, too. She clearly had some history there.

"Look," Kyra stammered. "We should really get going."

"What's so scary?" Alex asked.

While Alex and Kyra continued along the path, the once lively trees now shriveled and darkened. The birds grew quieter with each step.

Alex moved blithely as his heart beat a merry song. He could visualize the enchanting school in his mind: there would be a huge school, like a giant castle, just like in an ancient book he once read. Many students would be going to class, with the School of Fire the biggest college of all.

They reached the wizard school. Alex's mouth opened wide with a dazed look about him. The school lay in desolate ruins. Blackened wood still stood upright in a few areas.

"There it was—Hillcrest Wizard School," Kyra said, sighing. "Well, what's left of it."

Alex pursed his lips. "What happened here?"

Kyra stared blankly at him. "You don't know?"

A whiney scream came from the building. It appeared dwarf-like, something Alex once had run from before.

"I told you we shouldn't have come here," Kyra said. "This place was destroyed… burnt down by goblins!"

"Goblins?" Alex asked. "Why?"

"They've been searching for somebody."

"Who?" Alex asked.

"A brave wizard boy who shoots fire. They say he doesn't succumb to fear, but they've been breaking him down ever since, in order to make him weak and fearful like everybody else. The dark lord said to kill every wizard until he finds this boy. Now do you get it? Slowly, walk backwards."

As they walked backwards, a goblin turned its head directly at Alex and Kyra. It yelled, "Aauugh! Wizards!"

The bushes around them started to shake. As they

did, pointy ears began to lift out of them.

"Run!" Kyra yelled.

Alex ran for his life toward the gate. He wasn't sure who this wizard boy was, but if it was he, he was surely scared, and would gladly succumb to fear. The monsters were hideous, and the only successful thing he'd done so far was run away.

Alex heard Kyra stop from behind him. He turned and found several goblins grouped around her. They drooled and ground their teeth. He watched Kyra pull something from her pocket—a stick twice the size of his mechanical wand.

Kyra pointed the stick at the goblins, and yelled, "Incendiaries globus!"

To Alex's amazement, the stick lit up at the end, casting a large fireball toward the goblins. A few goblins collapsed from the blast, but about ten stood their ground.

Kyra pointed her wand to the ground between two goblins. She yelled again, "Incendiaries globus!"

A second fireball blasted the ground, knocking the two goblins on their backs.

While Alex panted and ran toward the gate, a goblin dropped from a tree and landed on its scaly feet. Alex stood still. It looked into his eyes with a nasty scowl and furrowed eyebrows.

"Aauugh!" it screamed.

"Aauugh!" Alex yelled back, though it wasn't any help. "Alright! You've got the wrong guy! I'm not a wizard! I just play with toys!"

Alex pulled out his mechanical wand. "See? It's just a toy!"

Alex gave a wide smirk. He pointed the mechanical wand toward the goblin, lit his lighter at the end, and pressed the button. A fireball shot directly at the goblin, which made Alex feel incredibly powerful, like a real wizard, but the cotton simply bounced off of the goblin harmlessly.

The goblin's face grew furious. "Aauugh!"

Alex froze. There was only one more thing to do: he threw the mechanical wand at the goblin's face. Clearly having no effect, Alex watched the goblin jump toward him. It stuck out its claws. Its mouth opened, revealing long, sharp teeth. Alex ducked, blocking his face with his hands.

As the goblin neared him, a thick hand of bark grabbed the goblin from the neck, and threw it against a tree. Alex tried to get a good look at his savior. The bark on its hands and chest left little room for doubt: it was Trin.

The goblin shook its head a little and stood up. It looked up at Trin in anger. The goblin stood and leaped toward Trin. Trin quickly drew out his bow, grabbed an arrow from his quiver, and shot it. The arrow flew steadily and pierced the goblin's chest, and it fell, limp, to the ground.

"Trin!" Alex said. "That was amazing!"

"Where's your friend?" Trin said.

"She's..." Alex turned, finding Kyra swiftly casting more fire spells at several goblins. "She's got it handled."

Trin nodded. "I'd say."

"How did you find me?" Alex asked Trin. "Oh, let me guess: the trees knew my location."

"You're learning," Trin said with a smirk.

"Wait a second." Alex frowned, crossing his arms tightly across his chest. "Why did you leave me on the road earlier?"

"Is this the time to talk about such things?" Trin asked.

"Yes," the boy insisted.

"Okay then," Trin said. "Our sources said the only way into the village was through its gates. Trees cannot walk among human settlements. And, considering our observations of emotional humans, it was best to leave without any distractions."

"What?" Alex said. "You could have said something!"

"I don't understand," Trin said.

"Alex!" Kyra shouted. She lurched toward them and nearly stumbled. "They're all dead. Help me!"

Kyra fell. Trin reached down in time to catch her fall.

"Were you hurt?" Alex asked.

"No," she said.

"What happened then?" Alex asked.

"I just need a moment to rest," she said, catching

her breath. "Casting magic doesn't just... come from the wand. It's an energy-releasing tool... it releases your own energy."

Kyra looked up at who or what was holding her. She narrowed her eyes at Trin above. "Is that a living tree?"

"His name is Trin," Alex said, smiling.

"Trees have names now?" Kyra asked.

Trin gave an awkward smile. "Hello!"

After a wide-eyed stare, Kyra fainted.

***

The morning's cool breeze slowly woke Alex. He opened his eyes and glanced around him. There was only burnt wood, and the partial ceiling above provided the only place with enough shelter to drag Kyra so she could rest.

Alex glanced to his left, and he saw Kyra sleeping near a burnt wall opposite him.

Something caught Alex's attention: Kyra's wand was halfway out her pocket. Smirking, Alex stood up and slowly wandered over to her. The burnt floorboards underneath felt rough, and its splinters were sharp, but the prize was just up ahead. Alex reached for her wand.

Prize in hand, Alex wandered down an outline of what must have been an old hallway. The scorched walls were barely standing in the area.

Alex's eyes locked onto the wand. It felt light, with a decent grip at the bottom. He wished he knew a spell to cast, but nothing came to mind. He tried to remember the fireball spell he heard from Kyra.

Alex shouted, "Incembiarum globbles!"

A yellow fizz came out from the wand.

His eyes widened. "Abracadabra!"

Nothing.

Why did it work before? Alex thought.

An unfathomable voice whispered from behind. "Alex…"

What was that? Alex thought.

Alex glanced around him, seeing nothing out of the ordinary.

"Alex…" There it was again.

Alex gripped onto the wand. His hand trembled. He lifted his arm, the limb suddenly heavy.

"Who's there?" Alex shouted.

A cold breeze swished him from behind. Shivering, Alex turned. A dark spirit, one with a face that looked like Governor Mallis, stood there in a black robe and red eyes. The spirit stared down at him.

Alex pointed his wand at the spirit. His hand shook even more—then it froze. An unseen force caused his still arms to fall to his sides. His body slowly lifted from the ground. As he levitated up into the air, Alex found that he couldn't move at all. He screamed at the top of his lungs.

"Alex!" Kyra yelled from behind.

Kyra ran closer to Alex. She struggled for the wand, but Alex wouldn't let go.

"I need it!" Alex shouted. "Behind you! I need it!"

"Need it for what?" Kyra shouted, as if she didn't see the spirit. "Give it back!"

Kyra pulled Alex to the ground. Alex could move again. He was sure Kyra saw his tears and pale face. Nothing loomed above them. The evil spirit was gone. Alex held onto the wand tightly as he shook and cried. As Kyra tried to pin him down, her hood fell off, the motion revealing her hair.

Alex froze. His eyes locked onto Kyra. As Kyra fixed her blonde hair, Alex couldn't help but stare at it. That was Anne's hair.

"What's the matter with you?" Kyra asked. "What happened? It looks like you saw a ghost!"

"I..." Alex tried to calm down. "I don't know. Anne?"

"I'm still not Anne," Kyra said, annoyed. "Why do you keep thinking I'm Anne? It looks like you were doing more than just looking at my wand. And it's not globbles, it's globus."

"Globus?"

"Incendiaries globus."

Just then, the wand shot a fireball toward the floorboards. They quickly rolled out of the way. The explosion created a huge hole.

"Oops," Kyra said as they both stared below. "Let's just keep that between us."

***

Alex followed Kyra down a sidewalk toward a residential area. His mind was far away. He wondered about the spirit he had seen that morning. He couldn't tell if it had been a dream or not. He used to pretend about wizardry, but everything felt so *real*. If he had the chance to tell his village he survived from real monsters, he would be famous, a hero!

However, no one remained besides the girl who went by the fake name Kyra.

"Wait," Alex said, "Where are all the wizards now?"

"Excuse me?" Kyra asked.

"The school," said Alex. "It's big, so there must have been many wizards."

Kyra slowed down, her eyes haunted by memory. "Well, several of them died just a few days ago. With the dark lord's help, the goblins threw everyone into the school..." Kyra's eyes grew wet, "and then the monsters burned the place."

"How?" Alex asked.

"The roof... it caved in on them. Not everyone died, though. The elders made sure the women and children escaped by teleportation through the empire for safety, but not many of the elders survived. I was one of those who escaped. That's why I've been wearing a hood, to conceal my identity."

Alex pursed his lips. "Because the enemy is out to

get us?"

"Us?" Kyra tilted her head as she studied Alex's face. "Wait a minute. Are you the boy the dark lord is looking for?"

Alex gave a shrug. "I think so."

"Come," Kyra said, wiping her tears. "I think you should meet someone."

CHAPTER 11
PROFESSOR KERR

Alex followed Kyra up an unstable flight of wooden stairs. The floor creaked severely, as if the wood was about to crack any minute. Worried, Alex gripped onto the railing. After a few more steps, they arrived to the third floor of the apartment complex.

When they walked through the third door on the left, the first thing Alex noticed was more creaking and groaning from the wooden floor. A crooked table supported a stack of worn, burnt books, with titles like *Alchemy of the Modern Day*, *Raising Children with Magic*, and *Combatting with Magic*. To his left he noticed another table that supported several plants, with a mortar nearby. Some boxes stood near a closed, dusty closet door.

"Do you live here?" Alex asked.

Kyra took off her hood. "It's not much of a wizard school, but it works for now."

"Works for now?" Alex complained. "Isn't there a second wizard school in case one gets… burned? The wizard school is supposed to be huge with lots of wizards, lots of students, food, classes, mostly food…"

"Well, this is what we got," Kyra said. "This way."

Alex followed Kyra to a small office. The wooden desk had trails of dried ink under several scrolls and papers. An elder, one with long gray hair flowing over his black robe, sat behind the desk. The elder held his wand in the air, casting a shiny light above him.

Kyra faced Alex. "Let me introduce you to the master wizard: Professor Kerr."

Once Alex walked closer to Professor Kerr, he knew he was truly going out of his mind. The man behind the gray beard and mustache was his grandfather!

"Grandpa?" Alex asked.

"Grandpa?" Kyra snarled. "He's not my grandpa. He's Professor Kerr. Show him some respect."

Kyra tried to get the old man's attention. "Professor, may I introduce Alex? He's interested in joining our school. A bad time, if you ask me."

"Hold that thought just for one minute," he said, waving his wand as he continued casting a bright light above. He beamed from ear to ear. "Why, look at that!"

Alex studied the light. It had a certain form about it. It was a yellow, transparent bird flying around in a circle.

Kyra turned to Alex with a low sigh. "You'll have to excuse Professor Kerr. One of the school's floorboards fell and hit him on the head. He's been a little aloof, to say the least."

"Aloof?" Alex asked.

"Weird," Kyra said. "Distant. The doctor said it might take him a few days to recover. I don't think he ever will."

No matter. The man's familiarity was rather calming to Alex.

Kyra cleared her throat. "Professor."

Professor Kerr's magic fizzled away. He turned to the children. "Yes? Why do you disturb me?"

"Again, this is Alex," Kyra said.

"Oh yes, yes," Professor Kerr said, facing Alex with a smile. "How do you do?"

"Good," Alex replied, trying to hide his smile.

Kyra hesitated. "Do you remember the wizard boy the dark lord is searching for?"

"Of course," the professor said. "All the countless lives the dark lord took to get to him." His face grew red as a fist tightened. "If I ever met that boy..."

Alex started to back away.

Kyra blurted, "Well, I think this is him."

The professor narrowed his eyes at Alex, and laughed in amusement. "The little boy with the poo-poo on his shirt? And you brought him here to me? Boy, why do you come here?"

"I want to become a wizard," Alex said.

"Ah," the professor said. "And does your family blood descend from a line of wizards?"

"No," said Alex, "I don't think so. My dad was an illusionist. He taught me fire tricks."

"No history at all?" the professor said. "Absolutely not! That would break the school code!"

"What school? Please," Alex begged. "I need to become a wizard to get revenge."

"Revenge?" Professor Kerr scoffed. "The greatest magic one could ever hope to learn is forgiveness, and you don't have to become a wizard to obtain such a skill. Forgive, and you will be set free from anger... from pain."

"But he killed my dog," said Alex, "and everyone else!"

"Oh dear," said the professor. "You'll certainly want your revenge then. What was the dog's name?"

"Professor," Kyra snarled.

Professor Kerr paused for a moment. "What was I saying about forgiveness?"

Kyra rolled her eyes.

"Everyone sought revenge against the dark lord," the professor sighed. "But his magic is far beyond our own, more powerful than we'll ever know. We all fear him, and it will not end well for you if you try. Save yourself. Go back to your family, and stay with them during this dark time."

Alex's eyes lowered and studied the floor. He wiped his nose, as said, "I don't have a family."

"Anyone else?" the elder asked.

"He killed them," Alex said, glancing up at the old man, quickly turning his gaze back down. "He burned my home. I barely escaped."

"I feel your pain," the professor said, apparently reconsidering his earlier insistence. "Our trainers are all dead. We cannot give you a proper education. But... even though you do not come from wizard blood, we may need the extra help. The road is not safe. No wizard is welcome in this land right now. And if they're caught, it means the penalty of death."

"I understand," Alex said.

The professor massaged his beard. "Kyra, why don't you train the boy?"

Alex glinted with excitement as he faced Kyra.

"That means years of training! I will not!" Kyra said. "He nearly killed me last night!"

"No, he did not," said Professor Kerr. "I was watching you with the Spell of See. You did excellent on your own. I must say your parents would have been proud of the young lady you've become. When Alex is ready, give him some practice at the same site. There's a great war coming, you know, which makes me believe this boy must be the chosen one to save us."

"Chosen one?" Kyra scoffed. "I've never heard of such a prophecy."

"Well, that's because I just made it up," he said as he laughed. "Now it must happen one way or the other. He was sent by the great Professor Kerr!"

"You need some rest, Professor," Kyra said.

Alex smirked. He liked the idea of being the chosen hero.

"Be nice to the young apprentice," Professor Kerr said. "That's an order, Kyra. Just because you progressed through the ranks quickly doesn't mean you get to be rude to newcomers. Give the boy five red credits for now. Get him some items from the inventory, and for everyone's sake, buy him some soap."

"What about the task you gave me?" Kyra asked.

"Never mind that for now," Professor Kerr said. "Your new task is to train the great chosen hero! Now where was I?"

Kyra rolled her eyes and walked away.

Alex stood frozen with disbelief. He was to become a wizard—a *real* wizard.

"Thank you, Grandpa... sir," Alex said.

Professor Kerr rubbed his chin. "For what, boy?"

Alex's smile grew wider. "I'm to become a wizard—a true hero!"

"Don't hold me to that!" the professor laughed. "I got hit on the head!"

CHAPTER 12
THE WAND OF ALFAINIA

Alex, with his shoulders back and a closed-mouth smile, watched Kyra struggle as she opened the closet room's door. Its creaky hinges echoed along with the floorboards' groans, a rolling drum matching rhythm with Alex's fast heartbeat. He had yearned for this moment for a long time, although having his apprentice ceremony in an apartment was unexpected. Even their presence felt unwelcome; the closet room's dust flew in anger from the disturbance.

"Welcome to the grand inventory room," Kyra said sarcastically, walking in with a sneeze.

Two clothing racks stood with a single aisle in between. Several black wizard robes in different sizes hung from the racks. In the back, a few thin blue uniform coats with white collars hung there. They looked considerably shorter, like they would end somewhere near Alex's knees. Against the walls were several burnt cardboard boxes.

Kyra continued, "The inventory room is not as big as the one we had at the wizard school, but these are all the uniforms and items that survived."

Alex followed Kyra down the aisle. The black robe

lengths became shorter as they walked deeper into the room. To Alex's surprise, they walked right past his approximate robe size. Curious why they were still walking, he shrugged and followed Kyra to the end of the room. He glanced back at the robes behind them. Kyra tilted her head as she stared at one of the blue uniform coats. It had long, loose sleeves and buttons that went downward along the right side of the chest.

"Here," Kyra said, pulling out a blue coat.

Kyra aligned the coat with Alex's shoulders, and saw that its bottom dropped to the kneecaps. She gave a slight nod of approval.

Alex glanced at the black robes behind him. "Can I have a wizard robe instead? All wizards have black robes."

"That may be true, but all apprentices wear these blue things."

"Why?"

"It makes it easier to spot apprentices," Kyra said, smirking. "Bullies especially loved it back in the school. If you want a black robe one day, there better be tales or songs written about you."

Alex reluctantly took the coat. He mumbled, "Do you have a black one instead of blue?"

Kyra shrugged. "At the wizard school, maybe—if you like burnt blue, of course."

Alex looked down on his clothes, and asked, "Should I wear this on top of these?"

"Who knows," Kyra said, tilting her head with

pursed lips. "As an apprentice, your enchanted, poop-stained shirt and trousers can actually be quite a useful defense."

Alex sighed. "Really…"

"I'm serious," Kyra said, smiling as she walked toward the door. "All people stink here, if you haven't noticed. Why do you think the dark lord hadn't burned this village down yet? We're the smelliest of them all—well, besides me. Anyway, it's time to go to the market."

"Okay," Alex said. "Wait. What about a wand? All wizards have wands."

"Oh, right…" Kyra said, as she turned to the boxes. She searched through the boxes one by one. While on the search, she pulled out some sandals.

"I don't know about the forest life, but you really need sandals, at least," Kyra said. She placed the sandals in Alex's hands. She went back to the boxes and searched for a wand.

"Here we go," Kyra said. She pulled out a wand. Alex felt light inside. It was old and brown, with visible cracks.

"An apprentice should use this," she said as she placed the wand onto Alex's held items.

"It looks used," Alex said.

"Yes," Kyra said. "This wand belonged to a slave. She became free and joined our school—quite the weak one, like you. Her name was Alfainia. She died using it."

Alex grew wide-eyed as he stared at the wand.

Kyra continued, "You'll get a better one later—if you don't die, of course. Most die. I don't want to give our best wands to people who haven't proved themselves yet, because they might die."

Alex looked up at her, and said, "But I'm the chosen one. All chosen…"

Kyra interrupted. "Well, according to Professor Kerr, the *chosen one* might as well be the chosen meal for a monster."

Although Kyra was serious, Alex began to chuckle. Kyra caught on and chuckled, too. Perhaps she was right, and there was only one way to find out.

***

Alex trailed behind Kyra down Main Street. The new sandals made it difficult to keep up with her, as it felt like he was walking on an unnaturally flat surface. He thought he did better without them, but because everyone else had footwear, he shrugged and scurried toward her.

The street was full of bitter memories. Nearby was the spot where Daryl kicked him out of the cart. Then two horse carts almost ran over him. Finally, he remembered Antonio, the child beggar, who stole his money and ran off laughing. In all, the street didn't bring back any warm memories.

However, there was a new memory: he had just

bought some used clothes—a white shirt and tan, cut-off trousers. They hid within his long, buttoned-up apprentice coat, though the trousers' ripped bottoms fell slightly beneath.

Alex thought the new clothes would impress the villagers as they passed by, but each villager failed to notice. His eyes wandered elsewhere. While walking near some food shops, he walked across a shop that made his eyes widen: *Radio Specialist Center.*

A 3D face appeared, talking through the window. The man wore layers of thin clothes with a rope-like cloth around his neck, disappearing beneath his shirt. Some text appeared below, which read *Representative Josh Karshner.*

"Let me repeat again," the representative said. "Before moving forward with the Emperor's request, we have reason to believe these documents, such as the Constitution, are forged, and it requires further evaluation before moving forward. Next question."

A transparent figure appeared to the right of Alex, dressed professionally in a tight suit. She looked at the representative through the window, and asked, "Does that mean Emperor Aydren may be returning to office?"

"We have the choice to ordain this youth back to office," the representative said. "His father was a very notable and great emperor, and we wish his family peace as they mourn his passing. But, given what his son Aydren pulled, innocent or not, we'll have to find a suitable, worthy replacement of his father."

"Excuse me," said another transparent businessperson to Alex's left. "You sound as if you're looking for a replacement right now. How do you know the documents were forged?"

The representative smiled cunningly, and said, "The evidence will be presented soon. I have no doubt about it."

"Alex," Kyra said. "We have to hurry."

"I'm hungry," Alex said, smelling fresh bread nearby.

Kyra sighed. "Well, all right."

After walking to a baking shop outside, Alex and Kyra stared at the bread on the table. He licked his lips.

"You!" said the shop owner.

Alex immediately froze. He recognized the shopkeeper's face, pointing at him beneath furrowed brows. She still had those gray eyes and matching gray dress.

She yelled, "Didn't I tell you to scurry along last time?"

Alex relaxed and gave a smirk. He reached into his pocket and lifted up a red credit.

The owner smiled widely. "So which one would you like?"

***

"Is it as you had hoped?" a voice said nearby.

"Hmm?" Alex said.

Alex concentrated on stuffing bread into his mouth while they walked down Main Street. He was chewing an unbelievable amount of doughy goodness. He knew the rest of his credits were going to go into the same warm, fluffy bread. He had no reason to ever leave the bakery.

"It is good to eat, actually," Kyra said, as she took a bite of her own bread. "You need energy to cast magic. As you saw earlier, if you cast too much magic, you can faint."

"I can't believe you fainted," Alex laughed through his full mouth. "I would never do that."

Kyra chuckled. "I fainted because of your talking tree friend. Where is he, by the way?"

"He appears when he wants to," Alex said. "I have no control over him."

"Don't you think that's a little strange?"

"No," Alex said. "Where are we going?"

"To the forest," Kyra said. "It's best to have you practice away from the village, I think."

"We can leave the village?" Alex asked.

"Of course," said Kyra. "If you know the right way. Hardly anyone does go out, though. Nature or materials—most choose materials. Though we'll have to stay close to the village to avoid any trolls, robot patrols, or other creatures out there. Then again, the smaller creatures are good targets for practice. We're almost near the…"

"Alex!" someone yelled. The voice sounded familiar—someone Alex's age. "Ciao, Alex!"

Alex turned to his left. A familiar olive-skinned boy beamed as he gave a long wave across the road. He wore the same oversized dirty-green sweater and cut-off trousers. A scarf was around his neck, and he wore his old-fashioned cap.

"Oh, no…" Alex whispered.

"What?" Kyra asked.

"It's Antonio." Alex replied. "Hold onto your credits. He's a beggar."

Kyra narrowed her eyes as the boy approached.

"Alex!" Antonio said as he ran toward them. A new bruise was found on his right cheek.

"Stay away!" Alex said, pulling out his wand from his long coat. "I'm a wizard now!"

"Apprentice!" Kyra reminded Alex. "And keep the wand hidden!"

Antonio revealed his empty hands, and then lowered them. "I was kicked out because I told you Mr. Ratzel's name. Oh man, I said his name again!"

Alex raised an eyebrow. "Why?"

"I thought you knew him," Antonio said. "He got angry that I said I was connected to him, and…" Antonio's words lumped in his throat. He looked down, rubbing his upper left arm as he winced.

"Are you okay?" Kyra said with empathy.

Antonio sniffed as his voice cracked. "He wants me

to find you, then bring you to him."

Alex gripped his wand even tighter, lifting it toward Antonio.

Antonio hesitated as he looked upward. "But I didn't come to bring you in! I wouldn't be honest about it if I was trying to trick you. Right? He said if I don't bring you back, he would come and find you, and then kill me depending on how he feels. I swear!"

"I'm guessing you both had some history together?" Kyra asked.

"Yes," Alex said, turning angry again. "He stole my credits!"

"Really?" Kyra asked, gripping her own wand.

"Wait!" Antonio shouted. "Look, I thought you were going to keep it for yourself. I'm sorry!"

Alex shrugged and put his wand away. "It's okay. I'm rich now."

"So what are you going to do?" Kyra asked.

"Yeah, now what?" Alex asked.

"I don't know. I can't go back." Antonio rubbed his left arm again. "I'd do anything to not go back."

"Why don't you just tell the authorities about Mr. Ratzel?" Kyra asked.

"Yeah," Alex said. "Maybe you can get some help."

Antonio shook his head, unwilling to make eye contact.

Alex pursed his lips and shrugged. "You can come with us."

Antonio looked up with beaming eyes. "Oh, I

would be most grateful!"

Alex added, "We're going to defeat the dark lord. Are you sure you're up to that?"

"Dark lord?" Antonio asked. "We… as in you and I?"

"The dark lord?" Kyra asked. "Alex, you're an apprentice—without a real trainer, I might add. The dark lord will have to wait."

Alex nodded at Kyra. "I know, but you can train me as we find him. Maybe we can fight goblins along the way. They should be easy."

"I'm good with a short sword," Antonio said. "I can buy one with the credits I still have. I never used it before, but I know how to swing it at monsters when I play. I never met a dark lord, but it sounds fun, as long as it's away from this terrible place."

"Then let's go," Alex said.

The two boys walked for the village gate.

"Wait!" Kyra said. "You can't just become a wizard in one day and defeat the dark lord!"

"We're not safe here," Alex said, glancing back at her. "We must go. It's perfect reasoning."

Alex continued, "You may deny it *Anne*, but we were once brave! You didn't have to hide with a hood on your head back then! You didn't have to hide behind a fake name! So come on!"

Kyra shook her head and stormed toward them. She mumbled, "Wait until I tell Professor Kerr about this…"

CHAPTER 13
WHEN A TROLL
RUINS YOUR LIFE

That sunny day, when nothing could possibly go wrong, Alex and Antonio playfully jogged down a beaten trail. An old wooden bridge waited just ahead.

Kyra stomped her feet from behind, and complained, "Seriously, we should stay closer to the village! We don't know exactly what we're dealing with yet, nor do we have any idea what's ahead on this path. Alex, you don't know how to pronounce a single spell. Antonio doesn't even know how to swing a sword. Can we all just stop for a minute?"

"Fine," Alex said, sighing as he stopped in front of the bridge. "What's going to make you happy?"

"Well, let's see," Kyra said, pursing her lips. "You should at least learn a spell or two."

Alex's eyes veered upward. "Incendyarus globbles?"

"No," Kyra said, "Incendiaries globus."

"Incendarious…"

Kyla growled.

"Why are these spell names so complicated?" Alex asked. "I once knew a single spell name that did it all for you. *Abracadabra*! Simple!"

"Life isn't so fun and simple anymore," Kyra said. "We've grown up a little faster than we should have."

"Says who?" Alex said.

"You," she said.

Alex pulled out his wand. "We'll see about that!" Alex pointing the wand into the sky, and shouted, "Abracadabra!"

Nothing.

Kyra laughed. "For a moment, I thought…"

"Abracadabra!" Alex shouted again.

The wand fizzled.

"Nice spell," Kyra smirked.

Alex shrugged. "It's supposed to do that."

"Alex…" Antonio shouted ahead with a trembling voice. "I think you should see this…"

Alex turned around and looked toward Antonio. "What?"

"Look!" Antonio yelled, pointing toward the bridge.

Alex's heart stopped. A giant monster, which wore a fur waistcloth over its scaly gray skin, stood ahead of them on the bridge. Its head was monstrously thick, and its sharp teeth and thick jaw made Alex shudder. The troll's teeth were just as sharp as the claws on his hands and feet. The monster stared down at them, licking its lips.

Kyra, turning pale, rubbed absently with her arms. "Alex, did you just conjure a monster with that spell?"

"I don't know," Alex said as he rapidly blinked. "I

guess *abracadabra* is kind of a generic spell name."

"What is it?" Kyra asked.

"My grandfather used to carve statues like this one," Alex said. "It's a troll."

"A troll?" Antonio asked.

"Don't run," Kyra warned.

Antonio asked, "Want to fight it?"

Kyra hesitated. "That is anything but a good idea!"

"Do you think we can take him?" Alex asked nervously.

"There's only one way to find out," Antonio said.

The group pulled out their weapons. Antonio gripped onto his short sword; Alex and Kyra pointed their wands at the troll. The troll only tilted its head.

"Go away!" Kyra shouted. "Or we'll attack!"

"Yeah, go away or we'll attack!" Alex yelled.

The troll spoke with a deep, slow, and gentle voice, "Why would you harm an old troll such as this one? This old troll has no means of causing harm. His stomach only asks for food, but his tongue struggles to decide who may be the tastiest."

"We are peaceful travelers," Alex shouted. "We just wish to pass by!"

"Pass by?" the troll asked, scratching his head as he drooled. "Now, you see, this troll would allow you to pass, but his stomach desires its toll. Yes, only two of you can pass. One of you must remain."

"Kyra would be more than happy to," Alex said.

"Alex!" Kyra shouted. "Why would you…"

"I'm joking," Alex said, chuckling.

"I say we fight!" Antonio said fiercely.

Kyra's wary eyes stayed glued to the troll. "I don't know about this. I've fought only small goblins before, never something of this size. I fear we would lose too quickly."

"Antonio," Alex said, taking a step back. "I don't think this is a good idea."

"What if we make a run for it?" Antonio said.

"It's too risky," Kyra said. "Trolls, as big as they are, would have no problem catching up with us."

"It's risky," Alex confirmed. "We're screwed."

"This troll's stomach begs for an answer," the troll said, rubbing his stomach.

"We can take him!" Antonio shouted, trying to convince Alex with a wave. "Come on, Alex!"

"Wait," Kyra said, "Only the brave can win. Alex, you're not brave, nor am I right now. But we could still have fun with this troll. What if we go with him to his camp for now? Then we can plan a strategy from there."

"Or just fight him now," Alex said.

"Let's go with him," Kyra said. "We don't stand a

chance."

Alex shrugged. "How did our first hour of an epic adventure lead to this? It hasn't even been an hour!"

"Antonio," Alex said in defeat, "We shouldn't fight—at least not yet. We should go with him."

Antonio lowered his sword as his eyes sunk. "Hey, troll dude, we'll go with you."

"But this old troll only requires one," the troll said, rubbing his belly some more. "But, if each one of his capture are willing to be eaten, then this troll's stomach will have an easy week."

"Then bring us to your camp," Alex said.

The troll scratched his head, and wondered out loud, "This old troll knows there's something wrong with this—maybe a strategy to fight him when he is not looking, but this old stomach just doesn't seem to care right now."

Snarling in confused excitement, the troll snatched up the children and hauled them away.

***

Below the bridge, iron chains shackled the children's ankles against the cliff. Alex struggled to ignore the stinging pain by staring across the dried riverbed. The troll, who sat against the opposite cliff, held both wands and Antonio's short sword. To the right of the troll was a large nest of bones.

"Hmm," the troll said, as it studied the simple, tiny

weapons.

Alex turned to Kyra to his left, and let out a deep breath that had bottled up in his chest. "Was this part of the plan?"

Kyra's eyes never moved from the troll. She shook her head slowly.

The troll tilted his head at Antonio's short sword. He shrugged, put the sword behind his back, and started using it as a back scratcher. He smiled at the sensation.

The troll moaned, "Back scratcher."

"Gross!" Antonio yelled. "Back stabber, more like it!"

"Antonio!" Alex hissed. "Be quiet!"

The troll stared angrily at the commotion, and then forgot about them as he tossed the sword into the nest of bones. The troll's eyes homed in on the two wands.

Antonio, who frowned at Alex, whispered in anger, "Look! He's breaking your wand!"

"Please don't break them," Alex pleaded. "We need them to kill the dark lord! To get my revenge!"

The troll snapped the first wand in half.

"Oh no," Kyra whimpered.

The troll snapped the second wand, causing Kyra to burst in tears. The troll roared, shaking the ground underneath them.

Alex tensed, worried, as he turned to Kyra again. "So, what's the escape plan now?"

"That *was* our escape plan," Kyra blubbered.

The troll tilted his head toward the shackled children, and licked his lips. "Which one to eat? This troll's stomach does not know."

Alex shouted with a shaky voice, "If you can't decide whom to eat, that would be fine, too!"

"Especially if you're dieting!" Antonio added.

"Quiet!" The troll roared, shaking the ground once more.

The troll got on all fours and crawled toward the children. Saliva trailed on the ground as it moved, and the steady stream of the putrid stuff poured onto Alex as it loomed over him. The boy closed his eyes tightly. He felt saliva streaming down his hair and cheeks. Alex peeked through half-closed eyelids, and found the troll staring at Antonio, eyes gleaming.

"Mamma mia," Antonio muttered.

The troll sniffed Antonio as drool oozed onto him.

"This one may do," the troll said.

The troll unlocked Antonio's shackles. He picked up Antonio by the ankles, flipping him upside down, the motion making his cap fall to the ground. The troll stood up to its full height, lifting Antonio high above the ground.

"Help!" Antonio yelled, and then, in his panic, reverted to his native language: "Aiuto!"

"Let him go!" Kyra yelled.

The troll opened his mouth, stuck his nasty, salivating tongue out, and moved it closer to Antonio. Then, to everyone's shock, the troll licked Antonio's sweater.

"This one has fur all over," the troll said, tasting the sweater's wool. His free, giant hand tugged on Antonio's scarf, and it sailed away, gracefully twirling to rest on the ground below.

"I'm not tasty!" Antonio yelled. "I don't even taste like chicken!"

The troll's sharp claws ripped at Antonio's sweater, revealing another layered shirt underneath.

"This old troll can smell tasty meat on this furry beast," the troll muttered, "but oh, so *little* of it!"

While the troll tugged at Antonio's sweater, Kyra closed her eyes tightly. Alex placed a hand on her shoulder, and whispered, "Kyra…"

"I can't look!" Kyra cried as her voice broke. "This is all your fault, because of that stupid spell of yours!"

Staring down at his hands, Alex felt his courage rally, looked up to the troll, and yelled, "Hey! Hey you! Pick my tasty meat instead!"

The troll froze. It gazed down on Alex with enlarged eyes, and asked, "Oh, why do you have to make this troll's choosing so difficult?"

"Why did you say that?" Kyra said.

"You heard what Professor Kerr prophesied," Alex said. "I'm the chosen one! Maybe this is what he meant—that I'd be the troll's chosen meal to save a friend!"

"What?" Kyra scoffed. "I added that as a joke earlier! You can't be serious!"

Much to Antonio's relief, the troll gently set him down. Next, the troll moved toward Alex. Alex noticed Antonio remained unshackled. He gave Antonio a significant look that tried to tell him to retrieve the sword from the nest of bones. Antonio understood, and scampered towards the pile of discarded remains.

The troll sniffed Alex. Air sucked into the troll's nostrils, pulling Alex's hair towards them.

"This old troll can finally smell pure, tasty meat," the troll said, salivating once more onto Alex. "This little beast is an outstanding choice!"

The troll unshackled Alex, and then grabbed him by the neck. Struggling for breath, Alex rose into the air. He struggled to break free from the tight grasp, but it did no good.

"This one, however, does have some fur," the troll said.

Alex gasped for air. He kicked and thrashed, knocking his sandals off his feet.

Alex's vision darkened. The last thing he saw was a sharp claw cutting away at his coat's buttons.

To his delight, however, his vision began to slowly come back. The troll let go of him. As Alex fell, he saw a blurry, bark fist slam against the troll's face.

Trin? Alex wondered.

Antonio, far below, hacked and slashed his sword against the troll's foot. The troll lost his balance and fell, still grappling with Trin. Antonio jumped away just in time. As Alex was falling closer to the ground, Trin's hand came down to slow Alex's descent. Alex rolled on the ground, headed directly toward a tree.

"Oh, no! Not again!" Alex said.

Alex hit the tree with a loud thud.

"Shame!" the tree shouted.

***

Alex woke up next to the tree that had thoughtfully halted his tumble. He heard muffled conversation from all around him. He opened his eyes and saw a blurry group of men walking around. There must have been twenty of them, each wearing linen robes and sandals. Their tan chest and arms each had several tattoos.

Two of the tattooed men dragged an unconscious, eight-foot man in animal hides.

Alex had a feeling that he had seen the eight-foot man before, and perhaps his imagination had turned him into an ugly, fat troll to fight. It was easier to think of him more as a troll than a madman who wanted to kill them.

A tall tattooed man knelt beside Alex. He held Alex's mechanical wand. The man nodded his head at the wand, and then met Alex's inquiring eyes.

"You awake now," the man said with a foreign accent. "Nice, this."

"It's mine," Alex said.

"Parents?" the man asked.

Alex stammered, "I don't know."

"Anyone?"

Alex shook his head as he thought of his grandfather. He didn't think Professor Kerr counted either—his grandfather wasn't a wizard. "No."

The man pointed to himself. "Then you belong to Jyd. This item… mine. Understand?"

Alex gulped.

A young boy in a linen robe ran up to Jyd. He had long black hair tied behind his head. He shouted, "Father!"

Jyd faced the boy with a warm smile. "What is it, Janik?"

"You called for me?" Janik asked.

"Oh, yes," Jyd gave one last look at the mechanical wand, and then he handed it over to the boy. "This… my gift to you, my son."

The boy's smile grew wider. "Mine?"

"Yes," Jyd said, then pointed to Alex. "He no longer need. You need for protection ahead."

Janik's eyes lowered to Alex's coat. "What about that?"

Alex shook his head, pressing his coat tighter to himself. His shirt felt rather rugged inside. He looked down on it. He was wearing his old, stained, smelly clothes.

"Where did…" Alex said, realizing he had neither money nor his new clothes. His long blue coat was apparently real, though.

"We prepare him soon," said Jyd, "then you have." Jyd handed Alex's sandals to Janik. "For now, this you have."

"Thank you!" Janik said, slipping into the sandals immediately.

"Those are…" Alex mumbled, but then realized he didn't care about the sandals at all. His eyes searched frantically around the area. "Where are my friends?"

"Friends, you say?" Jyd said. "One of them leave you then. We save." Jyd looked back to the dead man. "A madman, this. Now you… ours. We saved."

Just then, Alex spotted a few tattooed men examining Antonio in the distance. One turned Antonio's resisting head from the left and then to the right. Others were amused as they tried on his scarf and cap, as if they were for sale.

"Who are you?" Alex asked.

"We are Tribe of Janyer," Jyd said. "We travel from Kingdom of Desert region, east of your Western Empire region."

Alex buried his eyebrows. "Why do you come this far?"

"We protectors. No concern," Jyd said.

"Protectors?" Alex asked.

"No concern. You help by profit… with friend." Jyd stood up, keeping an eye on Alex.

"Protectors for whom?" Alex asked.

"Come, boy," Jyd said, tugging Alex by the arm.

"Not much time. Now, up!"

CHAPTER 14
FREEDOM GATE

Next morning at Hillcrest Village's northern gate, citizens hustled about the festival events. The northern gate was once called Freedom Gate, but after the empire besieged the American savage village, it was renamed to Lawrence Gate, in honor of the first emperor.

The festival was full of colors and vibrant display. Merchants sold exotic foods, knickknacks, souvenirs, and even various animals as pets or for labor. There were games and activities as well, including one stand that offered animal rides. Children ran by with beaming smiles with laughter.

To the right of the gate, a Janyer guard lifted Alex onto a large platform. Another set of calloused hands firmly positioned Alex to face an overwhelming crowd of richly dressed men and women.

With layers of chimney soot, ash, and grime washed away, Alex's sensitive skin prickled at the morning's breeze and fog. His icy feet felt rooted to the spot, and his elbows pressed into his sides.

Alex's wrists pressed against his only rag—a white linen waistcloth—similarly worn by rest of the captives on the platform. Men, women, and children, including Antonio, lined up to his left and right. While their eyes gazed blankly at the crowd or looked downward, Alex's eyes jumped from one to the other with an opened mouth. The crowd shouted as if Alex and the other captives were the new bread in town. Alex's lips quivered. His knees shook and pressed together.

"Four hundred reds!" a man in the crowd shouted.

"Five hundred reds!" shouted another.

Had Alex heard them right? Their eyes were glued to his, as if he was a piece of meat for sale. His toes curled. His eyes fell, studying the blurry platform below.

"Five hundred fifty reds!" an earlier bidder shouted.

Representatives of the Tribe of Janyer were standing to the left; their smiles grew wider with every credit increase.

Alex looked to his right. Some families were exiting the Lawrence Gate. One poor family, whose father pulled a wooden cart with all their belongings, had some children who jogged along and laughed as they played tag. With silent tears, Alex leaned toward the direction of the family.

"Six hundred reds!" another challenged.

While looking to the right, Alex saw Antonio standing on the far end of the platform. Antonio shuffled his feet, as he cowered slightly behind a tall adult captive.

All Alex could do was think of all the events that

led up to being a captive. He'd rather be exploring the festival with so many fun games and animals to see; instead, he *was* an attraction to see. He sighed, feeling defeated from his wizard play.

Overwhelmed, Alex turned aside and made a step toward the platform's exit. Calloused hands immediately grabbed Alex's shoulders and positioned him back toward the crowd.

Alex's blurry eyes searched the crowd frantically. He cried silently, "Mom… Dad…"

"Seven hundred reds!" Another said.

Alex's blurry vision caught a familiar adult in the crowd. There was something about the man's blushed face and heavy size. The man lifted his right hand, and shouted, "One thousand reds!"

The crowd grew silent. The man's voice allowed Alex to process the missing detail: it was Daryl! Daryl was the traveling trader who brought Alex to the miserable village, to help him travel to a wizard school that never was. Only one thing ran through Alex's mind: Daryl must have been there to free him! Alex wiped his tears away and waited eagerly.

"We have one thousand reds!" shouted what must have been the auctioneer. "Do we have another bidder?"

The crowd scanned for raised hands.

A shy elder among the crowd raised a shaking hand, and shouted, "One thousand one reds!"

Daryl glared at the elder, hands at his hips. He

shouted, "One thousand two reds!"

"Oh, rats," the man sighed. "I only have one thousand one reds."

"One thousand two reds!" the auctioneer said with an upturned face. "Anyone for—I don't know—one thousand three reds?"

The crowd laughed.

"Sold for one thousand two reds!" The auctioneer shouted. "Congratulations on your purchase, sir. With his age, I'm sure he'll last a long time. I invite you to the pay booth for your purchase."

"Move," a guard commanded Alex just behind his shoulder.

Alex nodded, obeying as much as he could to get to Daryl. He carefully stepped down the platform, guided to the pay booth. Daryl approached at the same time.

"Alex!" Daryl shouted with a shrewd smile. "You're the last child I thought would show up here."

Alex burst into tears as he wrapped his arms around Daryl. He blubbered, "I was so scared!"

"There, there," Daryl said, patting Alex on the head as his smile drooped.

"Wait," Alex said as he sniffled. "What about my friend Antonio?"

Daryl gave a quick, disgusted snort. "Antonio?"

"He's still up there," Alex said. "It's my fault he was captured. Please! We have to free him, too!"

Daryl glared at Antonio with a tight jaw. "I'm afraid I'm all out of extra funds… for things I care about, anyway. He's useless to me."

The cashier turned to Daryl. "Name, please?"

Daryl turned to the cashier, and answered, "Daryl Ratzel."

Alex's posture stiffened. He took a few steps back. With each step, he widened his eyes further at Daryl. Daryl turned to Alex and gave a light, cunning nod.

Alex remembered Antonio fled from a child-begging business run by a man named Mr. Ratzel. Moreover, he remembered Daryl said he was a businessperson, one whom Alex would be better off without.

"You're paid in full," the cashier said. He turned to an empire soldier. "Officer! Got another one for you!"

The soldier came by. "I'll update his arm chip."

With a timid breath, Alex watched the soldier scan his arm with a mechanical device with a handle at the bottom.

"It shows he's going to be a citizen of the empire by next year," the soldier said.

"He's an orphan," Mr. Ratzel said. "He just runs about the streets. Refuses orphanages."

The soldier turned to Alex. "Is this true?"

Alex gulped, unable to nod.

"Since he ended up on a slave platform, I don't deny it. I grant it." The soldier gave a quick nod to Mr. Ratzel. "Okay. I registered the slave under your name. His tracking number is 5-761-191, or just type in his name for his whereabouts, status, and so forth. The slave is all yours."

"Thank you," Mr. Ratzel said, turning his attention back to Alex.

Trembling inwardly, Alex watched Mr. Ratzel take a few steps toward him, and then the man knelt to eye level.

"Don't worry, Alex," Mr. Ratzel said with that same cunning smile. "I'm not going to kill you. What a waste of money that would be, if that were the case."

Alex stammered, "But you just freed me from… so why was I just…"

Mr. Ratzel shook his head. "No, Alex. Well, not after what you just told me. Just so you don't go blabbering about my business, you'll be working at my side for a while. Think of yourself as my own little assistant. You'll get a roof over your head. Come. We have some catching up to do. And I take it you hadn't found that magical wand yet."

Alex shook his head.

"What about Antonio?" Alex asked as he glanced back to the other captives. Antonio was at the far end, barely visible.

"Come on," Mr. Ratzel said.

Alex sighed. He followed Mr. Ratzel, but he kept looking back. Antonio wiped tears from his face.

"I'm sorry," said Alex, "but he's my friend! I can't leave him!"

Alex fled from Mr. Ratzel and ran toward the auction platform.

"Alex!" Mr. Ratzel yelled.

Swishing through the crowd, Alex made his way to the platform stairs, climbed it, and ran toward Antonio. Alex and Antonio caught each other's eyes. Before he could reach his friend, someone pushed Alex off the platform. He fell, and landed hard on the moist grass and soil below. Dazed, Alex looked up. On the platform, a Janyer guard glared down on him with cold eyes.

CHAPTER 15
HOMECOMING

Alex's right ear flared in sharp pain. Mr. Ratzel dragged him and Antonio by the ears down a dark hallway of weathered floorboards. A rugged wooden door stood ahead of them. Its cracked borders danced with orange and yellow light. Mr. Ratzel kicked the door open, and then threw Alex and Antonio into the small, dusty room.

While trying to massage his released ear, Alex gave the room a quick scan. There was nothing inviting about it. A few torches supported by sconces warmed and lit the room, with a small airway above. Its wavering light revealed only a thin, fur sleeping bag on the floorboards, and a little mouse hole to its right.

Several children with smudged faces and dirty rags stood outside the door. They watched the commotion with fear and curiosity.

Mr. Ratzel faced the children just outside the door. He shouted, "Stop watching and start begging!" He slammed the door shut on them.

Fumbling for the right words, Antonio spun around to face Mr. Ratzel, and shouted, "I... I was bringing Alex back like I said I would! I swear!"

"Liar!" Mr. Ratzel slapped Antonio across the face. The blow sent the boy spinning to the floor against the wall.

Antonio sniffled quietly, as if the extra company witnessing his shame made it worse than just being struck. Alex pressed his fist against his chest.

Alex approached Mr. Ratzel, and begged, "Really, he was bringing me here! Honest!"

"Really?" Mr. Ratzel asked, shaking his head slowly at Alex. "Even when you called Antonio your friend earlier today?"

Alex felt off balance. His eyes fell to study the spattered soil and grass around him. That's when he noticed boots storming toward him. A hand reached for Alex's throat and dragged him backward, pressing him against the wall.

"Tell me," Mr. Ratzel snarled, breathing warm air against Alex. "To whom did you share my business?"

"Nobody, sir!" Alex shouted, shaking uncontrollably. "Honest!"

"Tell me!" Mr. Ratzel yelled again.

"I didn't tell anyone!" Alex shrilled.

Being unable to further convince the man, Alex looked away and closed his eyes tightly.

Silence.

Mr. Ratzel smiled. "Good!" was all he said as he released Alex's throat.

Feeling relieved to breathe again, Alex fell to the floor. He looked up at Mr. Ratzel with inquiring eyes.

"I believe you," he said.

Alex lifted a single eyebrow.

The big man tilted his head back. "After dealing with so many children, you learn to tell who's lying and who's not."

He turned to Antonio on the floor, and raised his voice. "As for this one, he's never been a good liar! Makes me wonder why I keep him around for begging."

"Please!" Alex shrilled. "I'll stay here if you don't hurt him!"

Mr. Ratzel scoffed at Alex. "Who said anything about you being free? You're free from punishment. Still, I paid a lot of money for you today, even *without* buying Antonio for you! Both of you are going to be working twice as long and twice as hard."

Alex's stomach clenched. He wondered how he had descended to such a hell.

However, Alex relaxed slightly as he saw Mr. Ratzel lean back against the wall. The man took a few deep breaths as he crossed his arms. The giant overlooked the two of them on the floor, yet his relaxing muscles gave Alex some hope that the worst was over.

"What am I going to do with the both of you?" Mr. Ratzel wondered out loud. "I need beggars, not slaves! But as slaves, you can't leave like the others are free to do."

He sighed. "Well, the rule of slavery says the slave can buy his or her freedom. So, work hard. Do what you're told. Show your dedication, and you can earn your freedom over time—and my respect, so I don't have to hunt you down later." He shook his head. "I should make sure you both don't see the light of day again, but now that I have you here, you can choose to either keep your mouths shut, or..."

"I'll keep silent," Alex said, as his voice cracked with emotion.

"I will, too," Antonio said.

"Good." Mr. Ratzel faced Antonio. "As for you, Antonio, you're staying in here today to think about your actions. You're a fine beggar, but it's situations like these that keep getting you into trouble. Work toward earning your freedom. Though I'm sure you'll stick around again, as you always seem to do." He said, chuckling. "What can I say? The food is good."

Alex watched Mr. Ratzel pull out his keychain as he opened the door. Then the towering giant looked directly down at him.

"Alex," Mr. Ratzel said slightly calmer. "You're coming with me."

Alex stayed glued to the floor. He could feel his muscles tensing in every part of his body.

"Now!" Mr. Ratzel demanded.

Shuddering at the thought of not following directions, Alex scrambled up and followed Mr. Ratzel out the door. Upon exiting, Alex glimpsed at Antonio. The olive-skinned boy, leaning against the wall, gave him a slow nod. Alex parted his lips, but then Mr.

Ratzel closed the door between them, and locked it with a skull-shaped key.

***

Mr. Ratzel's horse cart bounced boldly along a lumpy forest trail. Shivering slightly, Alex crossed his arms, tightening Mr. Ratzel's gray cloak around his oversized shirt. He observed the rain pouring to his right. A wooden wheel below him turned with fresh, sticky chunks of mud and soil.

"Well, this must have been an awkward day for you," Mr. Ratzel chuckled. "But that's why I said Hillcrest Village has its own belly of secrets. Most of us just keep our business to ourselves."

Alex stared at Mr. Ratzel with narrow eyes. "You're a bad man."

Mr. Ratzel laughed. "Why is that? The children are free to leave as they please. They stay for food and shelter. Think of it like an orphanage."

"Then I…"

"You are a *slave*," Mr. Ratzel interrupted, "and so is Antonio. Maybe it's better that way for the time being. Don't have to worry about you two as much."

Mr. Ratzel took a deep breath and continued, "I wish you had your magical wand today. This is one of those days where it could have come quite handy."

Alex gave a long, low sigh. "I'm not a little kid anymore. Wands don't work. They're not real."

"Well, you almost fooled me about a week ago," Mr. Ratzel laughed. "What changed?"

Alex shrugged, his eyes wandering aimlessly at the passing trees.

"You'll be playing again," he said with a closed-mouth smile. "That's the nice thing about being so young."

Alex raised his voice. "How can I play when I'm a slave? When my family and friends are all dead?"

Mr. Ratzel pursed his lips, and then shrugged a shoulder. "What happened to them, if you don't mind me asking?"

Alex shook his head as he studied the trees again.

"Why did you leave me on the street?" Alex asked.

"You looked like a good kid," Mr. Ratzel said. "Shame it would be for me to put you in my little business." He shrugged. "I guess I could have, if I knew you were choosing to be homeless. I figured you'd come to your senses and go to the orphanage or find me. Since you obviously didn't go there, I felt compelled to buy you."

He continued, "I always wanted to design an orphanage that trains children to work hard for themselves... to prepare them for the real world. They learn to make coin. But here's the real kicker: why not throw all that money into a single collection?"

Alex gave a fixed stare. "Your collection?"

"You get food and clothes, don't you?" Mr. Ratzel asked.

"Your clothes," Alex said, looking down on himself. "They're too big."

"You'll get some of your own this week," Mr. Ratzel said. A warm smile overcame him. "Here we are!"

Alex looked ahead through the rain. A small, dilapidated house was noticeable just down the path. No other homes were around it. It had a wooden fence that went around the overgrown lawn, but parts of the fence were broken. It was hard to tell if anyone lived there.

"Here's our first stop," Mr. Ratzel said.

Several yards away, Mr. Ratzel pulled the horse cart aside.

"What am I doing?" Alex asked.

"Take anything valuable," Mr. Ratzel said.

Alex's brows pulled in. "But that's stealing. Stealing is wrong."

"Wrong, but necessary," Mr. Ratzel said, as he pulled an empty corn sack from the back. "Fail to do that, you'll be the next one locked up for a few days.

"But my church..." Alex said. "I'm not supposed to steal."

"Soon enough, materials will be your new religion," he replied. "You'll get along much better with the rest of the empire that way, at least with your new home here."

"Here you go." He handed the sack to Alex. "Take this sack, fill it up, and then bring it back here."

"You're coming in, too, right?"

"I'll be right behind you. Now go."

Alex nodded slowly. Taking a deep breath, he took off Mr. Ratzel's long cloak. He climbed out of the cart and jumped down to the squishy path below. Shaking his head and cringing inwardly, he took wide steps toward the house, trying to avoid as much of the muck as possible.

The house looked as if no one had lived there for years. Moss grew on its logs, and the windows were cracked. Alex stepped onto the rough wooden porch, which creaked loudly.

I can't believe I'm doing this, Alex thought.

Facing the door, he slowly turned the knob. The door opened. He leaned in and eyeballed the darkened room.

"Hello?" Alex whispered.

No reply.

Finding the silence a good sign, Alex quietly crept inside. The cold floor creaked with each step. The windows' lights revealed dust swirling and settling around the old furniture. An ancient couch sat against the wall. A crooked table stood at the far corner. Two cups of water rested on its surface. He approached the table.

A pair of hands grabbed him from behind! One arm wrapped around his chest, and the other hand sealed his mouth. Alex yelled for help, but it only came out as muffled grunts. A hand swiped the empty sack from his grip. Next, a pair of hands dropped the sack over his head, and pulled it halfway down his body. Arms wrapped around Alex's waist. Behind him came a throaty laugh.

"Have you had enough?" the man laughed.

"Get off me!" Alex yelled. "Let me go!"

The front door creaked open further. Mr. Ratzel said, "That's good enough, Tim."

The hands let go of Alex.

Alex pulled the sack over his head. He turned, his pulse racing.

Alex tilted his head. "Trader Tim?"

"This boy was too easy," Trader Tim said, laughing some more.

"He's a new one," Mr. Ratzel said. "Just bought the boy today."

Alex couldn't move his eyes. "But you're Trader Tim."

"That's me name," Trader Tim said with a hoarse laugh. "Rule one: never go through the front door."

Alex glared at Mr. Ratzel, waiting for an explanation. What was this? Alex was supposed to steal some items from a house, and just happened to run into Trader Tim?

"Alex, you learned what not to do next time," Mr. Ratzel said. "I wanted to see how far you would get. Go back outside and wait to try it again."

The boy's nostrils flared. "But you could have told me this was a test!" He turned to Trader Tim. "Are you in on this, too?"

"Are you expecting me to rhyme some words together for you?" Trader Tim said with a sharper tone. "What did my brother just tell you? Go! Wait outside."

Alex, rubbing absently at his arms, shook his head and stormed outside. Just as he did, one of the two brothers closed the door behind him.

The rain pounded against Alex's head, and all he could hear were muffled laugher and quiet conversation as they caught up inside. Without any idea what to do, Alex sat down, defeated, on the steps.

He waited for seconds, which turned into minutes, and then minutes turned into a deep sigh.

Why would they leave me outside in the rain? Alex wondered.

He shivered with his arms crossed, and the wind easily slid through his shirt. Maybe he deserved it. He was stupid for going through the front door, whispering, "Hello?" No burglar would ever do that, except for him. However, if they didn't throw him out there as a punishment, maybe they had done it so that...

Alex's posture straightened. He smirked as he got up. He ran around the house and headed to the back door.

***

Several minutes later, the front door of Trader Tim's house opened. Mr. Ratzel walked out as he laughed with Trader Tim.

"Where's the boy?" Trader Tim said.

Alex, sitting on the horse cart, listened in. Mr. Ratzel turned to the cart and locked eyes with Alex. The cart contained several of Trader Tim's bags, each filled with stuff. Alex tossed his chin back proudly, giving the men a knowing grin.

Trader Tim laughed. "Well, I'll be... You might want to hold onto that lad."

Mr. Ratzel pursed his lips, gave a closed-mouth smile, and nodded toward Alex. He said in reply, "I think I will."

CHAPTER 16
MR. TINKS

Within the small closet room that night, two torches warmed the backs of Alex and Antonio. They lay in front of the mouse hole.

"Here, Mr. Tinks!" Antonio whispered.

The swaying torchlight revealed a shadow of whiskers from within the hole. The boys beamed from ear to ear.

Alex, who had never seen a mouse, wasn't sure if the mouse was more interested in the water dripping from his wet hair, or Antonio's last piece of cheese. The two cracked plates weren't the reason, as only crumbs remained from their dinners. It had to be the cheese.

"I think he's just shy because you're new," Antonio said with crinkles around his eyes. He tilted his half-dried head, picked up the cheese from the dusty floor, and handed it to Alex. "Here."

Alex stared down at the cheese. "What do I do with it?"

"Bring it close to the mouse hole," Antonio said, "but not too close, because we want Mr. Tinks to come out."

Alex gave him a closed-mouth smile, and then chuckled as he rubbed his moist arm. "Okay."

He brought the cheese near the mouse hole and kept a grip on it. Mr. Tinks' nose came out again, sniffing the cheesy aroma.

"Come on," Alex insisted.

"We won't hurt you," Antonio said.

The mouse took a few steps outward, cautiously stepping as its nose sniffed onward. Alex brought back the cheese a little and set it down. The mouse launched forward. Sensing that there wasn't any danger, the mouse stood on its hind legs and gnawed hungrily at the cheese.

"Wow!" Alex said, smiling widely.

"Now Mr. Tinks has his dinner, too," Antonio said with a pleased look. He gently petted the mouse's fur. Antonio glanced to Alex. "Now it's your turn." Biting his lower lip, Alex stretched his right arm out toward the mouse. He cringed, noticing that the bottom of his drying arm had picked up some dust from the floor. Ignoring it, he used the palm of his hand to faintly brush the mouse's fur. The mouse didn't mind the petting as it ate. Smiling, Alex pressed a little harder against the fur.

Something pounded against the door, rattling it in its frame. The mouse—frightened by the banging—dashed into the mouse hole and was gone.

Antonio turned toward the door with a reddened face. "What?"

"It's bedtime, boys," Mr. Ratzel said through the door. "Did you have your baths and meals already?"

"Yes," The boys said in a sharp tone.

"Good," Mr. Ratzel said. "Get some sleep, for tomorrow will be a busy one. Antonio, you're begging the whole day tomorrow while I'm gone. Alex, you'll be coming with me. We'll talk more tomorrow."

"Yes, sir," Antonio sighed.

"Okay," Alex replied, brushing at his arm.

"Good night," Mr. Ratzel said.

"Good night," the boys replied.

Alex knelt upward. Dust clung to his stomach, arms, and legs. Sighing, Alex brushed at the persistent dust with his hands.

"Don't worry about it," Antonio said. He knelt on one knee, also with a light coating of the grime clinging to him. "The dust will help tomorrow when we're begging. The general rule is to clean every three weeks. It helps with business."

"Why clean at all, then?" Alex asked, shaking his head. The mouse hole grabbed his attention again. "Think he'll come back out?"

Antonio shrugged. "I doubt it. I'm sure we'll see him again soon. I'm always locked down here anyway." Antonio looked up at Alex. "So he made you steal from homes today?"

"Not really," Alex said. "Just some training."

"With Trader Tim?"

"Yes," Alex said. "You know him? I can't believe

he's one of us."

"Mr. Ratzel said there's a dark side to everyone," Antonio said.

"What if we flee?" Alex asked, climbing into his new sleeping bag.

"It's not so easy, not like last time," Antonio said with puffy eyes. "We're slaves now. Property."

"So?"

"So, now the soldiers know where we are at all times thanks to our arm chips. They'll throw us back in here. It's not worth it. And I don't want to get… hit again."

Alex pursed his lips with furrowed brows. "That's not right."

"Stay on his good side," Antonio said, climbing into his own sleeping bag. "Better get used to begging. I know I am."

Needing a moment to think, Alex sighed as he faced the ceiling above. The waving torchlight sickened his stomach. He remembered the flames all too well at home, and the sight of the inn's roof collapsing as the structure buckled from the blaze within. Whether it was his fault or not with the fire, Alex held his stomach, wracked with pain from the guilt.

"I don't feel good," Alex said.

Antonio yawned. "Well, if you're going to throw up, do it on *your* side."

"We were going to fight the dark lord," Alex said.

"We can't play in here," Antonio said.

"He's real!" Alex said in a sharp tone. "He burned my home down. He killed my friends and family. He made me flee to this stupid village."

"What's the dark lord's name?"

"Lord Mallis," Alex replied, and then shrugged as his voice cracked. "Governor Mallis."

"Governor Mallis?" Antonio asked. "That's funny. I mean... to think of him as a dark lord. Well, he probably is. You should get revenge."

Alex shrugged. "I tried. My wizard skills are useless. They're all imagined, anyway."

"If all you do is imagine, nothing gets done." Antonio grew lost in thought. "I mean, imagination is a start, but... it needs action. Because when Mr. Ratzel... all I do is..."

Alex shot up in his sleeping back as his eyes widened. "I know! You can turn in Mr. Ratzel because of what he did to you before being a slave!"

Silence.

"Antonio?" Alex asked.

Nothing.

Wondering how Antonio could fall asleep so fast, Alex leaned back in his sleeping bag and sighed. Instead of imagining his own escape, this time he imagined a better world for his friend. A faint smile spread across his face as he fell asleep.

CHAPTER 17
BURIED TREASURE

Alex, garbed in tattered rags, rubbed his icy neck as he approached the next adult. The cold, cobbled sidewalk kept his toes curled, his skin prickled as the dense, moist fog seeped through his rags. A few ghost-like horse carts trotted past hazy shops that were just opening up for the day.

Beggars roamed the streets in the morning. Some of them, often adults, were honest citizens and were clearly not part of Mr. Ratzel's business. Alex felt remorse walking by these truly desperate people, knowing they needed the credits more than he did, but the absence of credits would anger Mr. Ratzel. Antonio taught him what he could about street life the evening before, but Alex imagined being elsewhere instead – somewhere adventurous.

"Please," Alex begged as an adult walked by. "Would you spare me some credits?"

"Off with you!" the adult shouted, raising his hand as he walked off.

Alex shouted mockingly, "May God have mercy on your soul!"

Antonio, in similar rags, hurried out of the darkened shadows to Alex. "You're doing it all wrong!"

"Why?" Alex asked, hugging his chest for warmth.

"You need a story," Antonio explained. "Something people can relate to."

"How's this?" Alex acted out sarcastically in a fake accent: "Hello! I lost me credits and am too poor to buy me some shoes!"

"That's just dumb," Antonio said, smirking.

"Why?" Alex asked. "Then... like what?"

"Maybe that you're looking for your parents," Antonio said with a playful smile, "and that you need credits to find them. You want people to get the feeling they can help so they feel good about themselves."

"I am looking for my parents though," Alex said as his shoulders sagged. His wet, cloudy eyes beseeched Antonio for help.

"Keep that look!" Antonio exclaimed, smiling. "Go with that story!"

"Why?" Alex asked. "It's true."

"All the better," Antonio said.

Alex tilted his head, and asked, "What do you beg about?"

"Well, it's kind of stupid." Antonio said, rubbing his hands together. "I ask if they can give me credits so I can go to school. And I would go if I could. But, with work and all..."

"Maybe you still can," Alex said. "I would, too. I wish I paid more attention in school earlier."

Antonio shrugged, and then focused his eyes at

something behind Alex. "Okay, two people are coming from behind you. Remember what we talked about. Go!"

While Antonio ran back into the shadows, Alex turned to face the oncoming adults. They wore animal hides, as if they were travelers from the forest.

"Excuse me," Alex said with sagged shoulders. "I'm wondering if you can help. I'm looking for my par..."

Alex froze. The adults in front of him were no strangers. A man and woman, both with brown hair, had faces Alex recalled from years ago.

Alex, dropped his act, and drew some deep breaths as he rubbed his chest. "Mom? Dad?"

"Alex?" the lady said.

Seeing his mother burst into tears, Alex reached out for her. As they hugged, Alex felt the warm embrace of his father.

"Alex!" an adult's voice boomed in the sky. "Alex!"

***

"Alex!" a voice whispered loudly. "Time to get up."

Alex, still trying to embrace his parents in his dream, watched their faces slowly fade away. He rubbed his eyes and managed to open them half way, finding the torches above blinding, their dancing lights yellow and orange. His half-closed eyes found Mr. Ratzel knelt on one knee by his side. Alex rolled onto his back, closing his heavy eyelids again.

"Come with me," Mr. Ratzel said softly. "There's some work that needs to be done by the morning."

Alex yawned as he stretched his arms. "What time is it?"

"Early. About three in the morning."

Alex's eyes widened. "What?"

Sitting up, Alex looked to his left and found Antonio still sleeping soundly.

Alex's eyes narrowed at Mr. Ratzel. "Why do I have to get up and not him?"

"You'll find out," Mr. Ratzel said. "Now come with me. That's an order."

Sighing, Alex quietly climbed out of his sleeping bag. He stood up, the fire warm against his back.

Still half asleep, Alex followed Mr. Ratzel into the freezing unlit hallway. The hallway's floorboards sent chills up Alex's legs. Alex hugged his chest for warmth and rubbed his skin.

Alex looked ahead with chattering teeth, "Mr. Ratzel…"

"Shhhh!" Mr. Ratzel whispered.

Alex hadn't noticed the doors in the hallway until then. The rest of the orphan beggars must have been sleeping in them. He felt sorry for them, thinking about his parents. They wouldn't have left him as an orphan on purpose. Something had to have happened to them.

After reaching the far end, Alex followed Mr.

Ratzel down a small set of stairs.

"Now, what were you saying?" Mr. Ratzel asked.

Alex curled his toes on the steps. He complained, "I'm cold."

"That garment not warm enough for you?" Mr. Ratzel said. "Well, I'm not surprised at this time of night. There might be a blanket or two still down here."

Alex yawned, rubbing his arms. "What do you need me to do?"

"Inventory." Mr. Ratzel said, reaching the brick floor at the bottom of the stairs. "See those bags over there?"

A distant torch swayed in the basement, providing enough light to make out several bulky bags at the far end—the corn sacks Alex had taken from Trader Tim the other day. A few brooms leaned against an old, unmaintained fireplace.

Alex's toes curled tighter as they met the cold floor below.

"Wait here while I grab them," said Mr. Ratzel.

Alex did, staring at the floor as his legs quaked. Dust covered the floor, and an insect with several legs crawled across the room. Biting his lip, he tightened his crossed arms.

Mr. Ratzel carried the sacks, along with an empty one, and dropped them on the floor near Alex.

Alex had had no idea what happened after stealing things, but, apparently, an inventory was what came next. Kneeling on his side, Alex looked up at Mr. Ratzel inquiringly.

"We're continuing on with your training," Mr. Ratzel said. "Once you get a bag full of items, such as these, you need to examine each one. Is the item sellable? Then keep it by setting it in a good bag. If it is not sellable, throw it in the bad bag. Do you got that?"

Alex nodded, studying the room.

"I don't think you do," Mr. Ratzel said. He knelt down and reached into the first sack. He pulled out a shoe with a ripped sole. "Is this sellable?"

Alex studied the shoe. He shook his head.

"Good," Mr. Ratzel said, putting the shoe into the empty corn sack. "Use this one for junk. I think you get the idea."

Mr. Ratzel's eyes searched the room. "There." He pointed to the corner. "There's a blanket for you." The big man stood up, brushing his pants. "I'm heading to bed. I want this done by morning. Then you're coming with me."

Alex yawned again. "Where are we going?"

"To sell the good items, of course," Mr. Ratzel said.

"But that just takes one person," Alex said.

"Right," Mr. Ratzel said. "You'll be doing something else for me there."

"Like what?" Alex asked.

"Questions, questions, questions..." Mr. Ratzel said.

Alex bit his lip.

"It's better just finding out later," Mr. Ratzel said. "Less to worry about, and more time for me to sleep. Little piece of advice: don't try running off. Your computer chip in your arm tracks your whereabouts. Oddly enough, every slave tries it at least once. Don't be one of them."

Mr. Ratzel started to walk back up the stairs.

"Can I…" Alex's throat locked up.

"Go ahead," Mr. Ratzel said.

Alex rubbed at his skin. "Can I find some extra clothes in here?"

"Yes, check the bags," Mr. Ratzel said. "See if you can find anything that will make you look like a decent citizen tomorrow."

"Okay," Alex said.

"And if you get done early, sweep the floor with one of those brooms by the fireplace. Keep productive. And I want you looking your best for the trip, so clean up afterwards."

Alex, shaking his head, forced out a cracked voice, "Why can't I go back to sleep?"

"It's a busy day tomorrow," Mr. Ratzel said. "Or is tomorrow today now? Don't worry. You'll get some sleep during the trip. Good night."

Shortly after, the door at the top of the stairs closed.

Finally alone, Alex burst into tears. He wondered what he did to deserve such work. Wasn't Antonio the punished one? But no, it wouldn't be right for him to do this either. He wiped away his tears.

Alex, recalling the blanket, walked hurriedly to it. He picked it up, only to find that it was covered in more dust. He beat the blanket, and the stuff flew out in clouds, angry at its disturbance. Alex sneezed once, then again. No longer caring about its filth, he wrapped the warm blanket around him.

He sauntered toward the sacks. He sat on his knees and kept the blanket wrapped as much as he could around him.

Alex felt overwhelmed by the six giant sacks. He untied the first sack and dumped the contents onto the floor. He lifted a sword sheath from the pile. Curious, he gripped onto the sword's handle and pulled it out of the sheath. He stood up, knowing he just had to try it out. He hopped around with the blanket, swinging the sword at imaginary monsters.

"You want some of this?" Alex whispered loudly as he swung the sword again. "What about this?" Alex stabbed the air with the sword. He liked the grasp of it. Based on his judgment, the sword was in good condition. Alex dropped to his knees again with the blanket. He placed the sword into the sack of good items.

Alex scanned the pile again. A blue cloth caught his eye. He reached into the pile and pulled out what was an almost new long blue coat. He couldn't believe it— it looked just like his old apprentice coat!

"Another one?" Alex asked himself.

Long blue coats must be popular for Alex's age. He remembered a mother at an apartment complex asking him if he would like some used clothes. After saying yes, the mother invited him to a small closet to go through an aisle of her son's hanging clothes. Alex pretended it to be a wizard inventory room, as it was full of garments. The mother gave him his first lengthy blue coat and sandals. The mother wasn't Kyra, nor did she give him a magic wand. Alex made that all up, but he was all grown up now.

Shrugging, Alex stood briefly, dropped the blanket, and put the coat on. After buttoning it up, the bottom fell to his kneecaps. He enjoyed its warmth. He got back down on his knees and searched the pile for some more clothes, but only a few ripped shoes remained.

Searching through the pile was somewhat fun, although working at 3 a.m. was beyond awful for Alex. Maybe he could find a mechanical wand again, for old-time's sake.

Then he found an interesting box within the pile. Inside it were four black bracers.

"What's this?" Alex asked himself.

The box had in big letters: *Soar Bracers*. The instruction guide on the back showed how to apply the bracers to the ankles and wrists.

Alex smirked widely. "Well, I guess I need to see if these work."

Alex pulled out the bracers and secured them on his wrists and ankles.

Each one had a large button at the center. Assuming he had a good idea of the directions at this point, Alex pressed the button on his right wrist bracer. A buzzing sound swelled in volume, and then lessoned as a beaming force appeared around the button as a ball of light. Then the rubber tightened around his wrist! Uncomfortable with the tightness, Alex shook his arm around to get the thing off. However, when his arm extended, he *flew* in that direction! He sailed toward some boxes at the far end of the dingy room.

"Help!" Alex yelled.

He smashed into several boxes. More of them toppled over, some with fragile items shattering inside. Afraid, Alex tried to pull the bracer off. Nothing helped.

Unsure how it had happened, he still thought it was fun. One bracer seemed to work. Wanting to try again, Alex swung his arm toward the ceiling—though maybe that was a bad idea. He yelled at the top of his lungs as his right bracer tugged his arm two stories upward. The bracer locked onto the ceiling, leaving him dangling high above the floor.

Alex looked down and hesitated. He was afraid of heights. The floor looked as if it were sinking further below him. He squeezed his eyes tightly and looked back above him.

The door opened at the top of the stairs. A tired little girl peeked through, clearly wondering what all the noise had been. Alex locked eyes with her.

"What are you doing up there?" the little girl asked.

"Go back to bed!" Alex said.

The girl shrugged and closed the door.

Alex peeked below him, wondering how he was going to get back to the floor. Then he remembered the buttons on each bracer. He used his big toes to press the button on each one around his ankles. He lifted his left hand toward his right hand, and pressed the last one.

"Here goes nothing!" Alex said.

Each bracer lit up, like they were ready to go.

Alex pushed the bracers downward. He soared toward the floor. Thinking he was going to crash, he cringed as his muscles tightened. When he got to the floorboards, he stopped and hovered nearly an inch off the floor.

Alex opened his eyes as a beaming smile spread across his face. "I've got to get me some of these!" Alex said, chuckling. He looked ahead and saw the brooms. "Wizards have brooms!"

Alex pressed the buttons again to turn off the bracers, which made him drop to the ground. He got up, slipped the bracers off, and carried them to the brooms. He wrapped two bracers around a broom— one on the back, and one on the front.

Feeling his heart flutter, Alex turned on each bracer, which immediately tightened around the broomstick. The broom turned flat and hovered off the ground.

"Whoa!" Alex shouted.

Alex put the broom between his legs.

"I'm going to laugh if this works!" He pushed himself forward, and the broom started flying in that direction!

"I'm a wizard!" Alex shouted with joy.

There was one problem: he was heading toward a wall! Alex gripped onto the broom, turned it to the left, and barely missed the wall. However, he landed into the boxes again, hearing additional glass items shatter inside.

The door upstairs swung open. Mr. Ratzel rushed into the room and found Alex in many toppled boxes. He cringed.

Mr. Ratzel, quite furious at first, calmed down and gave a warm smile. He shouted, "I told you you'll be back to playing again!"

CHAPTER 18
THE RETURN OF BRAVERY

Alex hefted a weighty corn sack, his arms aching at the strain. His sore knees pressed firmly against the still cart's wooden edge. While lifting the sack, Alex's eyes searched far and wide for comfort, anything to take his mind off his labor. A few blocks away, a small group of children in long blue coats sat on the sidewalk and faced a teacher.

Alex was dumbfounded—the lengthy blue coats were school uniforms? Well, that made more sense than a wizard apprentice's coat. Maybe he can use it for both play and school. Being in the same uniform though, he wished he were with the students. He felt so out of place working for Mr. Ratzel.

Whether the sidewalk was the students' normal place for school or somewhere else, the sun was a good enough reason to stay outside. Its warmth spread throughout the village, and the shade of Mr. Ratzel's house made Alex cool enough. Mr. Ratzel, who must have seen his struggle with the sack, came toward Alex and pushed it upward.

"There you go," Mr. Ratzel said.

Alex pulled the sack over the cart's edge, letting it

topple among the other sacks.

Alex huffed short breaths as he looked down at Mr. Ratzel. "Was… was that the last one?"

"Yes, thanks to the immaterial gods," Mr. Ratzel said, wiping his sweaty forehead. "You got everything?"

Alex observed his clothes from below, smiling at his familiar wizard apprentice uniform again. He wore the long blue coat over his new cut-off trousers, and fastened to his feet were ankle-tied sandals. They felt like hard wood underneath him. He wanted to take them off, but Mr. Ratzel had suggested keeping them on.

Alex nodded.

"Good," Mr. Ratzel said. "Meet me up front and we'll be on our way."

Alex turned and carefully guided himself through the sacks and various boxes. Once he got to the front, he climbed over the lifted edge and slid into his seat.

"Beat you to it," Mr. Ratzel said as he smiled from his left.

Alex gave him a playful smirk, and then asked, "Where are we going?"

"To a small savage hamlet named Riverside."

"I have a friend who lives there," Alex said, smiling at his memories of Jack. "What am I going to do there?"

"What you have been doing: being my little assistant," said Mr. Ratzel. "While I'm selling items with everyone there, I'll have you search their homes."

Alex jerked his head back. "What do you mean?"

"What do you think I mean?" Mr. Ratzel said. "Stealing."

"From their homes?" Alex asked.

Mr. Ratzel scoffed. "You're a bright one today."

Alex shook his head swiftly. "I can't do that."

"You can, and you will," Mr. Ratzel said sternly.

"What if we get caught?"

"You'll just have to make sure it doesn't come to that," Mr. Ratzel said.

Alex shook his head. "No. I won't do it."

"Say that again and I'll slap you."

"I won't."

A hand thrashed across his face. Alex massaged a stinging pain on his right cheek.

"Say that again." Mr. Ratzel said.

Alex lowered his hand and looked fearfully at Mr. Ratzel, and then gulped. "I won't do it."

Alex thought he could move his head in time, but the slap was hard enough that his head throbbed, and tears streamed down his face.

"Again!" Mr. Ratzel said.

Alex sniffled as he lost eye contact.

"Need I remind you what you are?" Mr. Ratzel said. "You're a slave to the empire."

"No," Alex said, turning sternly at his abuser. "I am an American!"

He closed his eyes, expecting another blow to the

head. Nothing happened. Instead, he heard boots fall to the earth below. Dirt brushed around the cart, and then the brushing grew louder. As he looked to the other side through tightened eyelids, an arm grabbed him and pulled him out of the cart.

"You're coming with me!" Mr. Ratzel snarled.

"Let me go!" Alex shouted.

Alex's arm flooded with pain. Mr. Ratzel dragged him to the old house and forced him inside. The hallway grew darker with each step, until they approached the closet. Oddly enough, he felt more pain from the sandals than the grasp, but he walked onward. Once the door opened, Mr. Ratzel pushed Alex inside.

The torchlight revealed Antonio waking up in his sleeping bag.

Mr. Ratzel pointed at Alex. "I'll come back with your punishment later, as I'm falling behind schedule, thanks to you. Until then, you're staying in here."

"Antonio!" he shouted, shifting his attention to the other boy. "Why are you still in bed?"

Antonio leaned up from his sleeping bag. He tried to make sense of the commotion, but appeared dumbfounded. "I'm sorry. I must have slept in."

"I don't have time for this," Mr. Ratzel said. "I'll deal with you both later. And..."

The boys watched Mr. Ratzel walk over to the torches. He lifted each one out of the sconces, and then he turned to the boys. "Until you start behaving, you're sleeping in the dark."

"Wait!" Alex shouted.

Mr. Ratzel walked out with the torches. The door closed, and then locked. Darkness flooded the room, drowning the boys with its abrupt void.

***

The lack of light grew frustrating during the rest of the day. The darkness made Alex wonder if he had his eyes open or closed; he widened them just to make sure they were open, but no light or reflection confirmed it. Even most chimneys had some sense of light. There was only the smell of food down the hallway, which made his stomach growl. At least he knew his stomach existed in the dark void.

The wall behind Alex's back gave him something to ground himself, something to remind him that he was still in the physical world. He wanted to feel the floor as well, and so he worked on untying his sandals; its tied strings wouldn't loosen from his ankles, but it gave him something to do. It still felt unnatural to wear the things. He had no idea why he had wanted them so badly back home. His fingers felt up the strings for knots.

"I'm getting cold," Antonio said from across the room.

"Yeah," Alex said. "You can use my sleeping bag. You can put your sleeping bag into mine."

"Then you won't have one," Antonio said. "I'd rather be outside than being in this place. I bet it's warmer out there."

Alex found a knot along the right sandal. He started fumbling with it.

"What are you doing?" Antonio asked.

"I'm taking these stupid sandals off," Alex said.

"Why?" Antonio asked. "When he comes back, he's going to make us work."

"I can run away faster without them," Alex said.

"You're going to run away?"

"Yes," Alex said.

"But you'll get caught!"

"He hit me!" Alex shouted, and then tried to take a few breaths to calm himself. "More than once."

"You'll get used to it."

"No, I'm not going to get used to it," Alex said sharply. "You shouldn't either. We need to leave."

"Leave where?"

"I don't know," Alex said. "Anywhere but here."

"I would, but I'm not as brave as you," Antonio said. "I imagine being free in my dreams."

"You said imagination doesn't get you anywhere," Alex said, slipping off the right sandal finally. "There needs to be action. That's what you said! You need to turn in Mr. Ratzel!"

"But I'm a slave."

"Those kids he's forcing to beg are not!" Alex shouted. "And he hits you all the time—maybe even them, too, if he does me."

"Maybe you can do it for me."

"I can't," Alex said, feeling around the second sandal's strings. "I'm going to get my revenge on Lord Mallis once and for all."

"I want to report him," Antonio said, sighing, "but I don't know what he'd do to me."

Just then, they heard a key jingling in the door's lock. Alex stared in the direction of the sound. He hurried at his second sandal.

The door creaked opened. A flame entered the room, causing Alex to squeeze his eyes at the bright light. He could hear Mr. Ratzel's boots slowly stepping in. He tried looking at the man, finding a dark figure there that had difficulty balancing.

"Antonio," Mr. Ratzel said, burping. "Stand up."

Antonio stared at Mr. Ratzel and stayed down.

"I said stand up!" he demanded.

Antonio scurried out of his sleeping bag. He shivered as the warm fire danced near and away from his rags. Mr. Ratzel placed the torch on a sconce.

Mr. Ratzel towered over Antonio. "Name your punishment for not begging this morning."

"None, sir," Antonio said.

"Wrong answer." Mr. Ratzel shoved Antonio to the floor.

"Get up!" he yelled.

"No!" Antonio cried.

Alex wanted to flee, but he sat there with his fingers

frozen between his sandal's strings. He couldn't leave his friend. He couldn't leave him at the slave auction earlier, and nothing had changed since then.

"Stop hurting him!" Alex yelled.

Mr. Ratzel dropped to his knees.

"Get off of him!" Alex yelled.

Mr. Ratzel punched repeatedly, sometimes hitting Antonio, but often hitting the floor instead as the boy ducked his head. Alex cringed with each blow, and burst into tears.

"Stop!" Alex cried.

From the mouse hole came sniffing whiskers. Mr. Tinks snuck his way out. Then, to Alex's surprise, the mouse dashed toward Mr. Ratzel, jumped onto his shirt, climbed up to his neck, and bit his ear!

"Yes!" Alex cheered. "Go, Mr. Tinks!"

Mr. Ratzel fell backwards, yelling at the sudden pain. The mouse kept going from ear to ear, biting at what he could. He ran onto Mr. Ratzel's face, looked at him with its cute sniffing nose, and then bit his lips!

"Antonio!" Alex said. "Run!"

Antonio scrambled up to his feet and ran toward the door. He stopped by Alex.

"I'm going to do it," Antonio said. "I'm going to be brave like you and Mr. Tinks, and..."

"Great!" Alex yelled. "Now go!"

"Okay!" Antonio yelled.

Antonio ran out the door and down the hallway. Alex, unable to loosen his last sandal, stood up and began to follow.

"Alex!" Mr. Ratzel yelled from the room.

Alex ran as fast as he could. Then he remembered he needed his wizard gear, still in the inventory room. He couldn't leave without them. At the end of the hallway, Alex ran down the stairs. He ran to the far side of the room, only to freeze in place as he heard his name from the top of the stairs.

"Alex!"

With a timid breath, Alex turned. Mr. Ratzel stood at the door. He held a key in his hand.

"Oh, Alex, how did it come to this?" Mr. Ratzel said. "In any case, you're right where I wanted you for your punishment. No, I'm not going to beat you; I have something better. Since you did chimney work before, I kept a chimney waiting just for you. I just wasn't sure of the right time to ask you to clean it. That chimney right over there…" He pointed at the fireplace. "You are going to clean it fully before the morning."

Alex gazed blankly at the chimney. The chimney looked impossibly old, was and caked with soot and grime at the bottom. He almost heaved at the sight.

"Think of this as a time to reflect on your poor actions today," Mr. Ratzel said, walking out the door. "And I'm going to kill that mouse."

The door slammed shut.

Knowing he had no way to escape, Alex ran upstairs to the door. He tried the knob, but it wouldn't turn.

"Let me out!" Alex cried as tears streamed down his face. His knees felt light. His voice grew cracked, reduced to a defeated cry. "Let me out…"

Hearing no reply, Alex wept as his back slid down against the door. There was no way he was going to clean another chimney. He was determined to find the most unexpected, magical way to escape.

CHAPTER 19
THE GREAT ESCAPE

The fireplace terrified Alex. Its coarse brick mantel had severe burn scarring across it, as if to give a symbolic warning that only the brave should enter. Its legs extended down to a small concrete base. The base's moldy front edge was the least revolting. Alex gulped and dragged himself closer.

Inside the fireplace was a mixed mortar of black and silvery ash, charcoal, coal dust, and debris. Clearly unmaintained and unused in quite a while, the base appeared to have a life of its own. But it wasn't necessarily the bottom that made Alex nervous—it was what lingered above.

Reaching the small base, Alex turned and sat down on the edge. Reminded of his remaining sandal, he worked on the now visible knot, loosened it, and then untied it. He slipped the sandal off.

Taking a few slow breaths, Alex gazed at the flue above him. Usually the pale sky shined at the top of the flue, but in this one he saw only pitch blackness. The light had always been a tease, taunting him to get out and to be free, but he had never been able to reach it. The surrounding edges could be the reason:

clumped soot surrounded them. Even the slightest breath caused ash and soot to fall onto his cheeks.

Taking a few slow breaths, Alex gazed at the flue above him. Usually the pale sky shined at the top of the flue, but in this one he saw only pitch blackness. The light had always been a tease, taunting him to get out and to be free, but he had never been able to reach it. The surrounding edges could be the reason: clumped soot surrounded them. Even the slightest breath caused ash and soot to fall onto his cheeks.

Feeling some of the soot getting into his eyes, Alex ducked and scrambled out of the chimney base. He rubbed his eyes and brushed his hair.

"I hate this!" Alex muttered to himself, "Wherever I go there's a stupid chimney! I can't do it. I can't."

"Yes, you can," someone said in the room.

Alex froze. He knew that voice. It was a voice he had been longing for, for a very long time. Too curious, Alex turned around.

"Dad?" Alex asked.

Alex couldn't believe it: it was his father! His father had the vibrant garments an illusionist would wear. He was in his forties—the same age and looks Alex remembered from years ago. His smile stretched his brown beard, just as remembered, too.

The man smiled with a nod. "Hello, son."

Alex wanted to hug him, yet questions kept fogging his mind, thicker than any caked soot in a flue.

"How?" Alex asked, quickly scanning to see if there were other exits he hadn't known about. "You... You can't be here. You're not real."

His father pursed his lips and shook his head. "No, I'm not real."

"Then why..."

His father interrupted, "You know how to get out of here. I don't know why you needed to ask me."

Alex tightened his fists. "I think the soot on my face means that I..."

"You always come to quick conclusions," his father

said. "You miss what's just ahead of you."

Alex pursed his lips. "What's ahead of me?"

His father gave a light chuckle, and then faced what was behind him. Alex looked in the direction of his father's eyes. A broom hovered by the far wall.

Alex turned his eyes to his father, but he was no longer there. He smiled anyway. "Thank you, Dad."

Alex retrieved the broom from the corner and headed back to the fireplace. Flying up to freedom on it sounded like a perfect, yet frightening plan. He needed something to cover himself to avoid all the soot above. He turned, looked around the room, and spotted the old dusty blanket. After taking it, he ran back to the fireplace.

"Here goes nothing..." Alex said.

Feeling his chest pounding like a drum, Alex crawled his way inside the base. He put the blanket over his head and the broom's high tip. He pointed the broom up, towards the top of the chimney.

As the broom was getting into place, it scraped against the flue's edge. A large collection of soot fell, almost knocking him off balance. His feet gripped into the debris below.

"Let's do this," Alex said, smiling. "It's now or never!"

Alex bent his knees, and then he pushed himself upward. The broom went the direction he jumped, and sailed faster than he did. He held onto the broom for dear life; the ground was no longer beneath his feet.

Ash and soot tumbled upon Alex, but he held tightly onto the broom. The broom turned a sharp angle to the right, and he realized the flue had turned at an angle. He banged from side to side, breaking off chunks of soot that fell, most likely leaving a heavy cleanup job at the bottom. He knew one thing: this was the *only* way to clean chimneys.

Something frightened Alex, however: he was afraid of heights. Daring to look down, he saw that there was nothing but pitch blackness below him and his blanket and coat flapping from behind.

"Slow down broom!" Alex yelled. "We're going too high... too fast!"

As he figured, the broom ignored him.

Alex kept going higher and higher, until a sudden light appeared from all around him. The bumping and jostling came to a stop. He smelled fresh air.

Alex knew what this meant. He threw the blanket off. He was free, flying in the blue sky!

"WOOHOO!" Alex yelled. "I'm free!"

The village grew smaller and smaller below him. Alex looked down, seeing miniature buildings below.

"I'm free!" Alex shouted again.

A light came on from the broom's Soar Bracers. It read: "Warning! Elevation too high!"

But Alex kept shouting, "I'm free! I'm free! I'm…"
He looked down with a widened mouth. "I'm afraid of
heights!"

Alex turned the broom almost straight downward.
He sailed, descending from the sky, the buildings
growing taller and wider below. He found the same
chimney coming straight at him!

"No!" Alex yelled. "You will not have me!"

Alex pushed the top of the broom upwards, and he
avoided the chimney just in time. Wanting to be closer
to the ground, Alex lowered his broom's high tip
again. Soon, he was flying over horse carts and the
soldier's hovercycles along the streets.

"Yeah!" Alex yelled, beaming. "Woo!"

Alex flew at a thrilling speed past a few soldiers and their parked hovercycles. They turned their heads in amazement. Unfortunately, they then jumped into their hovercycles, kicked them on, and shot forward as they flew into the sky.

Alex looked behind him, finding the hovercycles closing in.

"Oh, man," Alex muttered.

Alex leaned forward, causing the broom to pick up speed. He flew between several buildings, and then turned sharply at a corner, toward a dark ally. The broom almost smashed into a building's wall, but he turned it enough to narrowly avoid the collision. Surprisingly, he felt the Soar Bracers taking charge when it came too close to the wall. He smiled wider as he turned one corner, and another corner. He must have lost the soldiers. He looked behind him. They were still behind him!

"Time for Plan B!" Alex shouted.

He closed his eyes tightly, and then pulled the broom's top upward. He yelled, "Signora, non-wizards!"

Alex sailed so high into the sky that he was afraid to look down. When he got enough altitude, he pushed the broom's top slowly down, until he leveled with the ground. He was high, and he had no idea where he was going.

Alex peeked below him. There were no signs of

hovercycles. However, he did see Hillcrest Village from underneath. And there was one more area he recognized in the distance along the mountains: Winter Brooks, the home of Lord Mallis.

Knowing the right direction now, Alex flew downward at an angle. He flew past Hillcrest Village and toward a grassy area leading toward the trees. To his surprise, he saw the terrible men that had sold him into slavery: the Tribe of Janyer. They looked like they had weapons on them, like they were marching for war. Ahead of them and marching in the same direction were several American savages holding weapons.

"Really?" Alex asked.

He had the distinct impression that the Tribe of Janyer and the American savages were on their way to some kind of war. He remembered the voices teleported from the radio, and wondered if these people had joined forces to fight for... well, freedom.

Alex noticed that the tree monsters followed the army from behind. Among them, Trin looked at Alex and gave him thumbs up!

"Freedom!" Alex shouted, soaring closer to the army.

Alex knew he had to reach Winter Brooks ahead of the army, but there was something he knew he had to do first. As he flew closer, there was one particular person he was interested in finding: Janik. There he was, holding Alex's wand... and Alex's lighter... and

Alex's… well, never mind the coat. He leaned forward, soaring as fast as he could toward the boy.

"Look at my new weapon, mom!" Janik said, beaming widely, hopping around excitedly. "There are cotton balls in it. I think I can put this lighter in front of it, and… when we see those empire baddies…"

"I'll take those!" Alex said, streaking past him. The items left Janik's hands. Alex looked back, shouting, "Thank you! You can keep the coat!"

Janik stopped, crying out loud, "MOMMY!"

Alex beamed at the return of his mechanical wand. As far as he was concerned, he was now a *real* wizard.

He pressed forward, flying toward the major city. It was where his parents went, it was there where Lord Mallis lived, and it was where his revenge awaited him.

CHAPTER 20
LORD MALLIS

Alex's apprentice coat flapped through the air. Wind brushed through his hair, but he kept his eyes on to the land below as he flew on his broom.

Winter Brooks grew bigger every few seconds; the city appeared as if people flew on brooms as well, but as Alex got closer, the brooms turned out to be colorful curved boxes. Each had four wheels, just as Mr. Ratzel's horse cart, but they were much smaller, and no horses carried them. They followed invisible roads in the sky, as if they were following a system designed to work in order. Alex enjoyed the freedom of his flying broom, laughing at the contrast between his unencumbered movement and their tightly controlled traffic.

"Oh no," Alex said.

Just below, he noticed an army leaving Winter Brooks. They consisted of large hovercraft like his broom, only much closer to the ground, and much heavier—and, no doubt, deadlier. Soldiers dressed in black walked alongside them. They must be preparing for war.

Alex noticed goblins and huge trolls following from

behind, marching irregularly in a scampering tidal wave of rancid bodies.

Just as he was hoping that he could slip past them without being seen, Alex spotted a troll roaring as it pointed up at him. Some of the hovercraft lifted further off the ground. Did they think he was a spy from the savage army? He shrugged. It must be awkward finding a spy flying on a broom.

"Land your... uh, broom!" shouted a ship through an intercom. The voice faded for a moment, as if someone was asking in the background, "Is that a broom?"

Knowing Alex had to lose them, he leaned forward, causing his broom to move faster toward Winter Brooks.

"We have an unidentified flying object entering the city!" another person said.

Alex soared on, passing the walls of the city. The city was spectacular: he had never seen something so rich and vibrant. Citizens shopped along the packed city streets, and huge towers attempted to reach the heavens. Massive billboards displayed the latest products, including Soar Bracers. Alex smiled at the sign. A few churches found below appeared old and abandoned.

A missile flew toward Alex. With wide eyes, he leaned to his right. He didn't make it in time. Instead, his bracers picked up on the incoming target, juked to the right, and the broom narrowly avoided the missile.

It sailed past him.

"Pull over the broom!" someone shouted from the hovercraft.

"No!" Alex shouted. "Get your own broom!"

Alex pressed the top of his broom down. He began sailing down toward the city. He leaned into the dive as much as he could, but then noticed he was heading toward a street loaded with shoppers. He pulled up as much as he could, leveled with the street, and then crashed through a stained glass window.

Hundreds of glass pieces fell, shattering on the dusty floor below. Alex, with no control over the broom, let go. He fell, and landed hard on the ground. The broom flew further into the building, and he watched where it went. It stopped near the far wall. Alex's attention left the broom. The inside of the building mesmerized him.

Dust flew around the windows. The sunlight lit a broken altar at the front. Broken statues lay all over the floor. They weren't like his grandfather's wooden carved statues—these were white. A huge cross lay face down on the ground.

Alex stood up, blinking a few times as he gazed up front. Finding the courage, Alex walked closer to the front. He recognized the altar and the cross from home. They would have services in the inn, but it looked nothing like the building he was in; it appeared as if abandoned for ages. Several newspaper ads were on the ground, as though homeless people slept there.

"What happened here?" Alex asked himself.

Several footsteps walked in the far back of the church. Alex turned. More than ten soldiers stood there with their guns pointing directly at him. As they slowly crept behind him, Alex slowly drew out his mechanical wand.

"Drop the weapon!" a soldier yelled.

"You first!" Alex yelled.

"It's a child," said a heavily-built soldier. "Drop your weapons."

"Seriously?" another soldier shouted.

"Just do it!" the heavily-built soldier said. "That's an order!"

With some heads turning to each other in confusion, the soldiers did what they were commanded. With each gun dropped, Alex gripped onto his wand even tighter.

"We did what you asked!" the heavily-built soldier said. "Now drop your weapon."

"Not until I see Lord Mallis!" Alex shouted.

"Lord Mallis?" he asked. "You mean Governor Mallis?"

"Yes!" Alex shouted.

"Why?"

"He destroyed my home!" Alex shouted, sniffling. "He destroyed my life!"

"You do know your weapon is useless, right?" the soldier asked. "Drop it. We want to *help* you."

Too sad about home to argue further, Alex's

shaking hand dropped the mechanical wand to the ground.

"Got it," another soldier said. "According to his chip, his name is Alex Waycrest. He's a slave of Daryl Ratzel."

"Alex Waycrest?" the heavily-built soldier said. "Get the governor on the hologram."

Wondering why the soldiers were surprised by his name, Alex's fists tightened as they worked on some devices. They set a round gadget on the ground, and then, in a matter of moments, Governor Mallis appeared out of thin air!

"What is it, Officer Braxton?" Governor Mallis asked. "And hurry—I don't have much time."

The heavily-built soldier, apparently named Officer Braxton, replied, "This is Alex Waycrest. He's the boy you've been looking for."

"Alex?" Governor Mallis said inquiringly.

Just then, Governor Mallis turned into the familiar dark spirit, and the soldiers turned into goblins awaiting orders. Their teeth ground as saliva drooled from their lips.

Alex quickly picked up his mechanical wand.

He put his lighter in front of the wand, lit it, and shot fireballs toward Lord Mallis a few times. Each one went right through Lord Mallis and fell to the ground below. Some of the goblins stepped onto the fires to put them out.

Alex stood there breathless.

"Enough, Alex," Lord Mallis said, turning back into his regular human form again. "I know you don't understand our technology, but I am not in this building. I am somewhere else."

Alex added, "So you teleported here by magic."

Governor Mallis smiled. "I've been looking for you, Alex. I had a feeling you'd find your way to this great city."

Alex wanted to speak, but he backed away instead.

"Don't be afraid," Governor Mallis said. "You keep running, and I'll have a hard time chasing you down."

"How can you tell me not to be afraid?" Alex said. "You destroyed my home! You killed my family!"

A few goblins crawled out from the back doors, their eyes glaring at Alex. The governor slowly walked toward him as his eyes turned red and his clothes formed into a black robe.

Alex backed off. "Stay away!"

The dark lord tilted its head, and then took a few steps back. The spirit faded away, revealing Governor Mallis again.

Governor Mallis sighed. "I'm sorry if I frighten you, Alex. I've been trying to find you, for the chance to apologize for what I did."

"What?" Alex asked, not believing him.

"When I saw you flee—you, an innocent child—I didn't... I didn't fully grasp what I had done—or if it was the right course of action to take. I wept, wondering if you would forgive me."

"Forgive you?" Alex asked. "I will *not*! I hate you!"

"Then please understand what led up to it," Governor Mallis said. "I saw you escaping the hamlet, and realize now that you must have been trying to explain the event to yourself ever since. As you probably know, the country is in a big transition right now. We burned some villages to the ground—you must understand, only to keep both citizens and savages in line. In other words, we used fear as a tactic to keep the people civilized through the uncertainty during this time. I shouldn't have done it. I shouldn't have killed those people." He massaged his weary eyes with one hand. "Seeing you that night, watching me, *witnessing* what I had done... It made me realize that I was deserving of your hatred."

"I don't care about your reasons!" Alex yelled. "I will never forgive you!"

Governor Mallis fought back some tears. "Alex, please. I can't make up for what I have done, for the lives I've taken, or for the pain I've caused you. But... I can't be trusted with power any longer, either. Too much authority was in my hands, and I was desperate to keep it. But I'm letting it go. I'm resigning as governor." He drew in a shaky breath. "I knew I had to find you. Your name registered recently under Mr. Ratzel. I know I can't fix the past, and I know my apologies are hard to hear right now."

Every word that the governor spoke caused Alex's fists to grow even tighter. The goblins came closer as saliva dripped from their sharp teeth.

Alex tightened his fists, and yelled, "I won't forgive you! I will never forgive you! I hate you!"

Alex stormed toward the governor, who shifted into the dark lord again. If the spirit was from Alex's imagination, he didn't care. It was the same target. "I hate you! I hate you!"

Alex pounded his fists against the dark lord's chest, but each blow went through the hologram. Some of the goblins jumped on him and pinned him to the ground. Alex screamed, trying his hardest to push aside the goblins as their red eyes towered from above.

"I hate you!" he screamed again as tears streamed down his cheeks.

Through his tears, Alex imagined spirit-like people circled around him. They were the villagers he grew up with. They had warm smiles. There was a peace about them, a peace Alex didn't know or understand. Anne was there among them, smiling. His grandfather was to her right, next to Mrs. Pembleton, and further down was Mr. Nutter—who shook his index finger left and right with his shaking head, of course.

Whether they were there or not, Alex closed his

eyes and cried. It was no use struggling. Defeated, his muscles slowly relaxed. He wished so much that he could go back in time with his mechanical wand and make everything okay and happy again. But it wasn't okay. And he wasn't happy.

He was defeated. The dark lord had won.

The dark lord's red eyes and black robe slowly vanished until Governor Mallis stood there again.

"Officer Garrison," the governor said.

An officer, apparently a goblin from Alex's imagination just a minute ago, turned and faced the governor. "Yes, sir?"

"Return the boy to his home, and do what we have discussed for him," the governor said. "What's done is done. Be sure to get him some new warm clothes and food for the journey."

"Yes, sir," the soldier said.

"I'm sorry, Alex," Governor Mallis said. His voice sounded very weak, tired, and defeated. "Go on home. You won't see me again. Honestly," he added, as the hologram began to flicker, "I don't think there's much left to see."

With that, the hologram faded, and disappeared entirely, leaving Alex alone with the soldiers, his rage, and his grief.

CHAPTER 21
ANTONIO

Soldiers slammed a battering ram against the door to Mr. Ratzel's house. The resisting wooden door defended itself with billows of dust. Unmoved, the soldiers rammed the door again. This time, it flew open. Soldiers rushed inside, guns pointing into the clouds of dust.

Antonio, across the street, wore an oversized soldier's black coat. He stood on his toes to see the commotion. It was by far the coolest thing he had ever seen. A smile grew across his face.

Victims of the child begging business lined up inside the front room. A few soldiers calmly got down on their knees and questioned each one. Soon enough, Mr. Ratzel came out of the house with his hands cuffed behind his back.

"I demand an answer!" Mr. Ratzel yelled as he resisted. "What is the meaning of this?"

A soldier responded, "The charges are running an illegal orphanage and forced child labor."

Antonio really wished he had reported the abuse, too, but he had been too scared to do so. Antonio caught Mr. Ratzel's eye. As the big man passed him, his glared at Antonio, making him shudder inside.

Mr. Ratzel warned, "If you say one more word to them, I will find you!"

Antonio's eyes fell. His knees trembled.

As the soldiers walked off, one soldier heard the discussion. He stayed behind and walked up to Antonio. He asked, "Do you have anything else we can use to charge this man?"

Antonio wanted to tell him about the abuse he had to endure, but each time he began to do so, he froze. He breathed timidly, lowered his eyes, and shook his head.

"Are you sure?" the soldier asked.

Antonio nodded.

"Alright," the soldier said with a faint smile. "Well, thank you for your bravery today, Antonio. You did good work. Keep the coat, buddy."

As the soldier began to walk off, Antonio breathed harder and leaned towards him. Not caring anymore, he ran up to the soldier, and grabbed him by the arm. The soldier turned around in surprise. He smiled down at the boy.

"Yes?" the soldier asked. "Do you have more to tell me?"

With quivering lips, and with tears forming, Antonio nodded again and again. His eyes would not leave the soldier until his witness streamed down his cheeks.

Antonio felt the soldier's embrace. They sat down

together on the sidewalk, and Antonio shared his story as his tears streamed endlessly.

CHAPTER 22
HOME

Alex wiped away a few remaining tears in the back of the horse cart. He overlooked the dirty path as the cart rode further away from Winter Brooks.

"Meat?" a soldier asked up at the front, lifting a piece toward Alex.

Alex barely heard the soldier, his mind far away. He had the dark lord, sort of, but he couldn't help feeling fooled by the governor's teleportation techniques.

They were bringing Alex back home. The remaining sunlight revealed a shriveled, dead forest along the path. He wore empire's clothes on top of his own: a thick, warm cloak wrapped around him, and comfortable traveling boots.

"Suit yourself," the officer said, lowering the meat. "We'll be there in a short while."

A voice startled Alex in the back of the cart. "I think I'm ready to tell you now."

Alex quickly turned to his left. Kyra was sitting next to him in the cart. He blinked his eyes, but she was still there.

"Kyra?" Alex said. "You scared me. How did you get on here?"

"Duh. You put me here because I want to say something," she said. "You asked before if I was Anne."

Alex pursed his lips. "Are you?"

"Of course!" Anne said, smiling. "Who did you think I was?"

"I knew it!" Alex said. "You looked just like her... because you *are* her. Why did you keep it a secret from me?"

Anne shrugged. "I like giving a shocker at the end, just like when we would imagine our grand adventures together. You know, you were right."

"About what?"

"I was hiding from my own identity because I wasn't brave enough," Anne said. "I want to be brave again. I want to be me. I don't want fear controlling my life anymore. Alex..."

"What?"

Anne lowered her eyes. "I have to go."

"Go where?"

"Alex, I'm dead."

"No," Alex said, shaking his head. "We're on an adventure together still."

"That adventure is over," Anne said. "It's time to let me go."

Alex's vision grew blurry. "I know, but I don't want you to go."

"You're going to find new friends for new adventures to come," Anne said. "You'll be fine."

Alex nodded, though he was on the verge of tears.

"Can you do a few things for me then?" Alex asked.

"Sure, what?"

Alex choked on his words. "Tell everyone that I miss them, and... if they can forgive me."

"Of course they forgive you."

"And," Alex said, studying Anne's eyes.

Anne leaned in closer.

Alex continued, "If you want..."

"Alex," Anne said with a smile, "I can read your mind, you know."

She leaned in, giving Alex a simple kiss.

"I hope the real Anne would be okay with this," Alex said.

"I think she would," Anne said, kissing him again.

The soldier, who was riding the cart, overheard Alex's conversation. He looked behind him and found Alex, by himself, kissing the air. He shrugged and looked forward again.

Anne leaned back. "I have to go now."

"Okay," Alex said.

Anne stood up, smiled at Alex, and then jumped out of the cart. She looked back and gave him a wave.

"Hey Alex!" she shouted, pulling out a golden wand. She pointed toward the dead trees off the path. "Abracadabra! Come on!"

Alex tried to listen again.

"Abracadabra!" she shouted, smiling.

Alex imagined a wand in his hand, and there it

was—only now he held a true wizard wand. He pointed at the trees around him, putting on his brave, smiling face. He shouted with her, "Abracadabra!"

The dead trees around them rumbled the ground. The trees started showing signs of life again—leaves and new branches sprouted until greenery flourished on every single tree. Life was beginning again, both outside and in Alex's heart.

As the cart turned along the curved road, Anne's wave and smile disappeared.

***

An hour later, the cart's wheels rode through mud below. What once was dirt and grass became ash and burnt wood. Feeling a few rough bumps, Alex opened his sleepy eyes, leaned up, and viewed his surroundings.

They had arrived at a burned hamlet. A few homes were barely standing. The inn no longer stood. He only knew it was the inn because of the outline of its dimensions on the bottom. The horse cart slowed down to a stop.

"Is this it?" Alex said.

"This is it."

"I don't understand," Alex said. "Why did he bring me back here?"

"My orders were to bring you here," the soldier said.

"Why?" Alex said. "There's no one here."

The soldier raised a brow. "Did Governor Mallis tell you what he did for you?"

Alex shook his head. "No."

"Well, the governor removed your name from the empire's database and cleaned up your records, as a gift. The empire knows nothing about you again. However, that *does* turn you into a savage again."

A smile broke out across Alex's face. He didn't know what to say.

"Off you go," said the soldier.

"Wait! You're not bringing me back?"

"Why would I do such a thing?" The soldier smirked. "American savages have a certain grudge against the empire, right?"

Alex stared at the soldier blankly, but then returned a wide smile. Wanting his savage role back, Alex carefully stood up on the cart. His new boots still felt strange and heavy, but he kept his balance as he climbed off.

"Governor Mallis offered a sack of food to help you get started," the soldier said. "Here you go."

The guard tossed a sack to Alex.

Alex looked down on it, and his stomach responded faster than his thoughts. He couldn't remember the last time he had eaten.

But then he reconsidered, and made up his mind, certain that he would do the right thing.

"He can keep it." Alex handed the bag back to the

soldier. "I don't want anything from him. I work for my food. Even for this." Alex reached for his cloak and pulled it over his neck. He threw it onto the cart.

"And these…" Alex sat down on the grass and mud, and he had a bit of a struggle, but he pulled off each boot. He got up and tossed them into the cart.

The soldier gave a warm smile. "Spoken like a true American."

The soldier pointed to the sky. "Look!"

Alex turned the direction the soldier pointed.

"Can you see the sun setting?" the soldier asked.

"Yes," Alex said. "What about it?"

"Six more of those and this whole region will take the next step to being American," the soldier said. "That is, if the Declaration of Independence and such prove to be real. Soon, we won't be divided. The governor thought you would want to be an American again before the rest of us. I would take that as an honor, if I were you. You and I stand for the same future. Take care, lad."

"Wait," Alex said. "Do you think the documents are real?"

The soldier shrugged. "I can't say for sure. But one can only imagine."

The cart's wheels began to turn. Alex backed up and watched the cart roll away as it squished through the mud.

The growing silence of the distant cart made Alex feel alone. His haunted past surrounded him, only to remind him of the cold air that seeped through his clothes.

A coyote howled in the distance. Alex's neck hairs rose.

Pressing forward, Alex trudged through the muck. The mud soon turned to a grassier area, next to the burnt inn.

Alex welled up in tears. He realized he wasn't truly home—he stood in an open graveyard.

Alex knelt close to the outline of the fallen inn. Not knowing what to think of what he saw ahead, his face fell, only to lean inward. He sniffed and breathed harder.

Unsure of what to say, Alex cried out, "I'm sorry. I can't find an answer… I tried revenge…"

Alex remembered a distant memory of Professor Kerr:

"Revenge?" Professor Kerr scoffed. "The greatest magic one could ever hope to learn is forgiveness, and you don't have to become a wizard to obtain such a skill. Forgive, and you will be set free from anger… from pain."

Giving in, Alex cried out to Governor Mallis, "I forgive you!"

As Alex grew tired, he yelled again and again, "I forgive you! I forgive you…"

Alex's heavy eyelids eventually won. There was something peaceful about his closing eyes, a feeling of contentedness, with the calmness of breath. He fell asleep, and it was the most peaceful rest he had had for a long time.

***

A cool wind brushed against Alex, and he found himself waking up near the inn. It felt like morning, as the sun's rays felt warm against him, and the birds sung lively songs to a new morning.

Alex leaned up from the grass. In a sitting position, he crossed his arms against his chest.

Alex listened harder. The birds weren't the only sound he was hearing. To Alex's right, in the near distance, he also heard a dog barking.

"There's not a single radio in these parts," an elder said in the distance. "I followed you and your nose, but I'm afraid we're just going around in circles now!"

Alex gave a wide smile. "Grandpa!"

Shooting to his feet, Alex listened for the direction of the voice. The voice was convincing and real.

In the distance, Alex spotted an elder man and a dog walking toward the hamlet. It had to be them!

"Grandpa!" Alex shouted, making a mad dash toward them. "Max!"

The small dog, clearly Max, *his* Max, barked as it ran toward him.

Reaching Alex, Max ran in circles as Alex reached his grandfather.

"Grandson!" his grandfather shouted, more joyful than the day he had bought his radio.

"Is it really you?" Alex asked.

George asked, "Do I have a radio in my hands?"

"No."

"Then it's me," George laughed. "Can't imagine Grandpa without one! Come here, boy!"

Alex grabbed his grandfather and hugged him tightly. Tears fell. He held his grandfather all the tighter.

Alex looked up, trying to make sense of what had happened. "How did you escape? I saw everyone go into the inn."

"No, no... not everyone," George said. "You see, Max, the ill-advised pooch, scampered off. I left the line to find him. From the looks of it out here, he saved my life. So, I guess all three of us had some time to explore the land."

Alex nodded.

"Good," George said. "So, now that you've been around, where is the nearest radio shop?"

Alex only smiled. His shoulders relaxed, his eyes closed in peace.

Regardless of where Alex's parents were, he knew one thing as he held his grandfather tightly: he was home.

ABOUT THE AUTHOR

 **Phillip Vaira's** passion for storytelling has led him to directing films and writing books. *The Sandwich Days*, an independent family short film he directed and co-wrote, was awarded Best Comedy Short for a Northwest Film Maker at Eugene International Film Festival in 2010. It has since been contracted for film distribution, and is used to raise awareness about school bullying. The light-hearted humor and drama from his earlier works carried over to his first children's book: *The Imaginary Wizard*. Phillip is currently in his fourth year of teacher certification with a literacy endorsement.

The author can be reached at philvaira@gmail.com.

Get Connected Online

for free wallpapers, games, the latest news, and more!

Official Facebook Page
www.facebook.com/ImaginaryWizard

Official Website
www.ImaginaryWizard.com

67311643R00140

Made in the USA
Charleston, SC
09 February 2017